Thanks to Thalie for the proofreading.
Thanks to Alec Longstreth for the colour advice.
Thanks to everyone at the Geslepen Potloden studio.

RADIGUÈS

STIG & TILDE

VANISHER'S ISLAND

NOBROW

London | New York

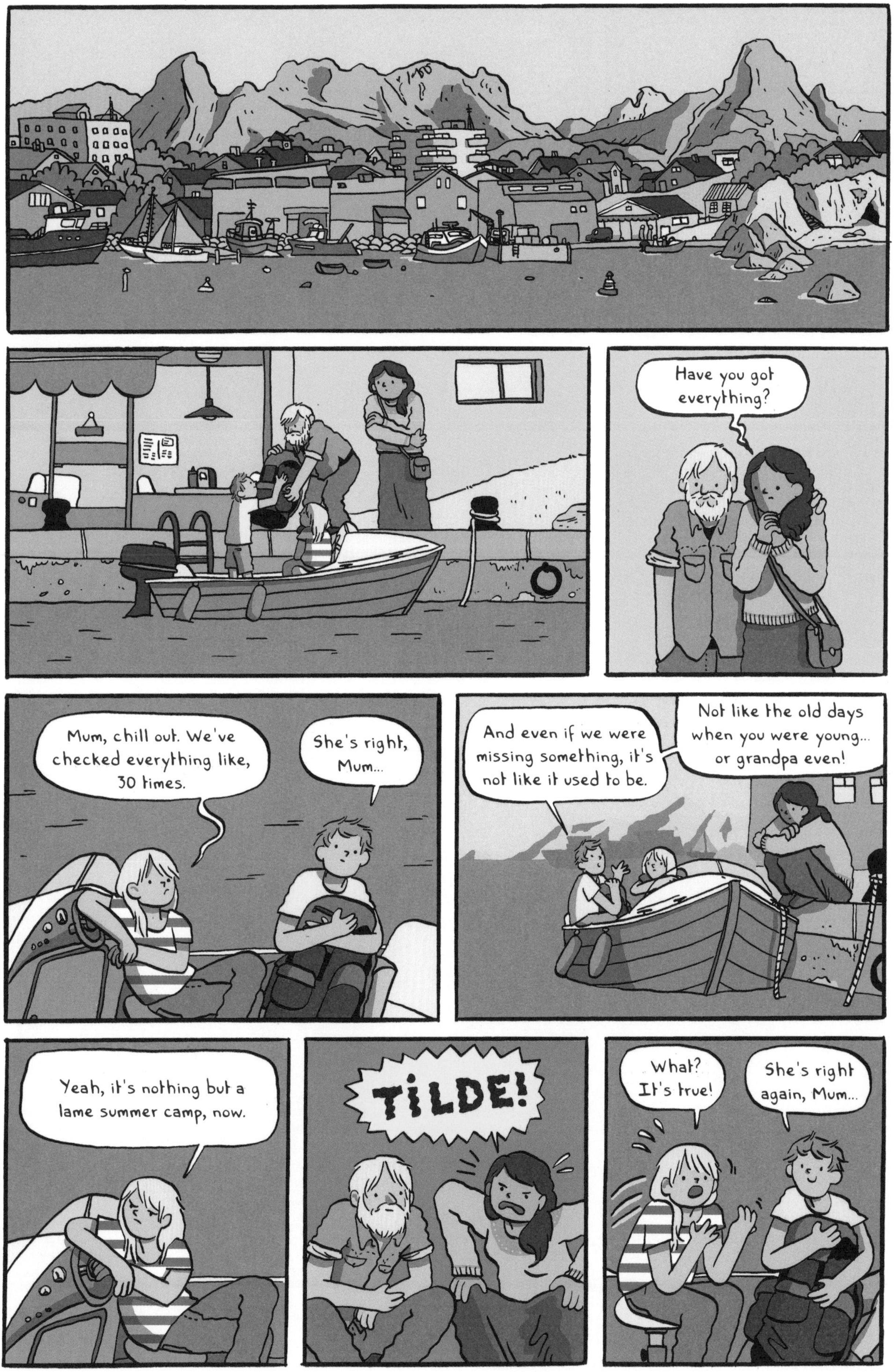
Have you got everything?
Mum, chill out. We've checked everything like, 30 times.
She's right, Mum...
And even if we were missing something, it's not like it used to be.
Not like the old days when you were young... or grandpa even!
Yeah, it's nothing but a lame summer camp, now.
TILDE!
What? It's true!
She's right again, Mum...

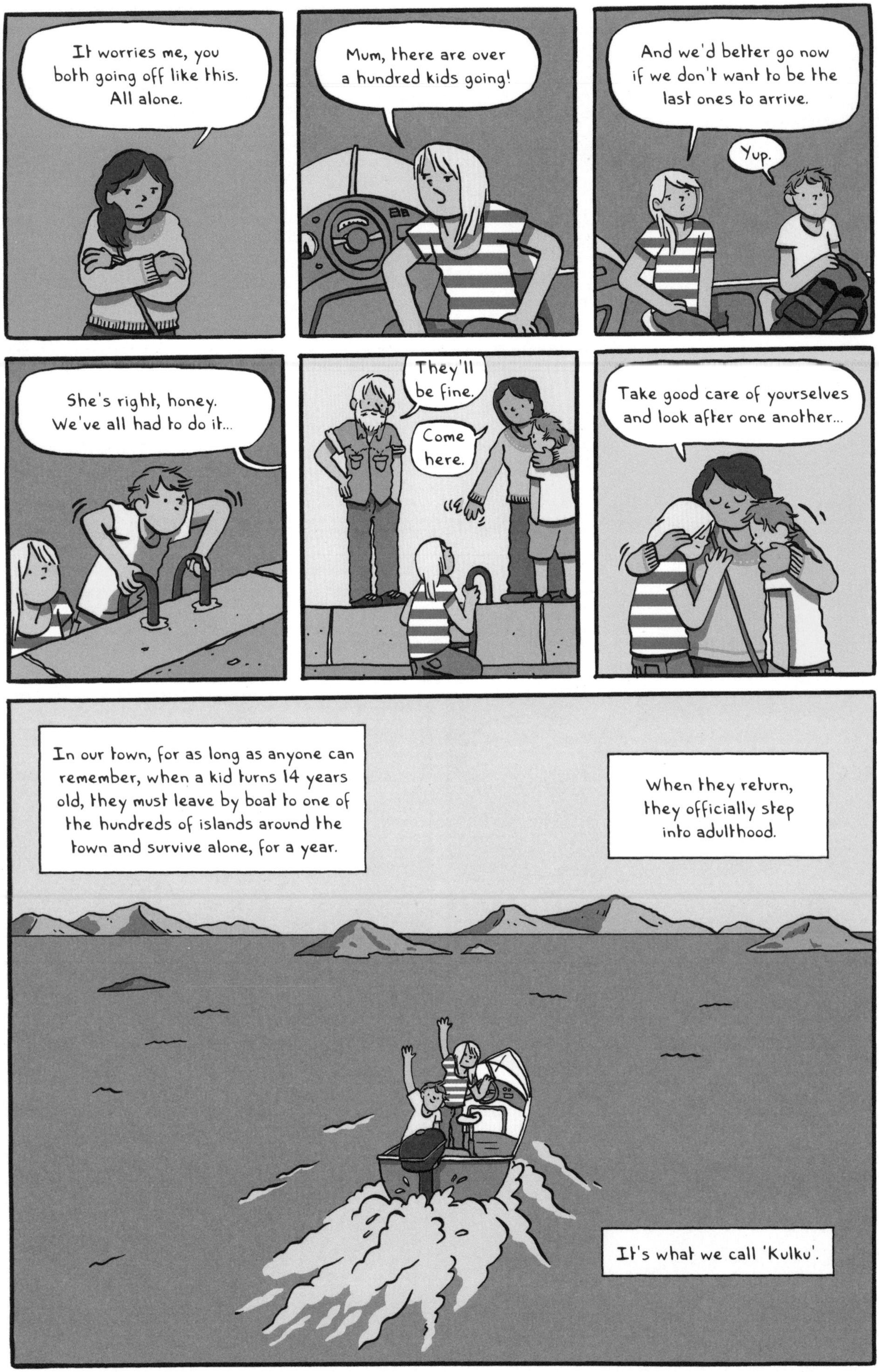
It worries me, you both going off like this. All alone.
Mum, there are over a hundred kids going!
And we'd better go now if we don't want to be the last ones to arrive.
Yup.
She's right, honey. We've all had to do it...
They'll be fine.
Come here.
Take good care of yourselves and look after one another...
In our town, for as long as anyone can remember, when a kid turns 14 years old, they must leave by boat to one of the hundreds of islands around the town and survive alone, for a year.
When they return, they officially step into adulthood.
It's what we call 'Kulku'.

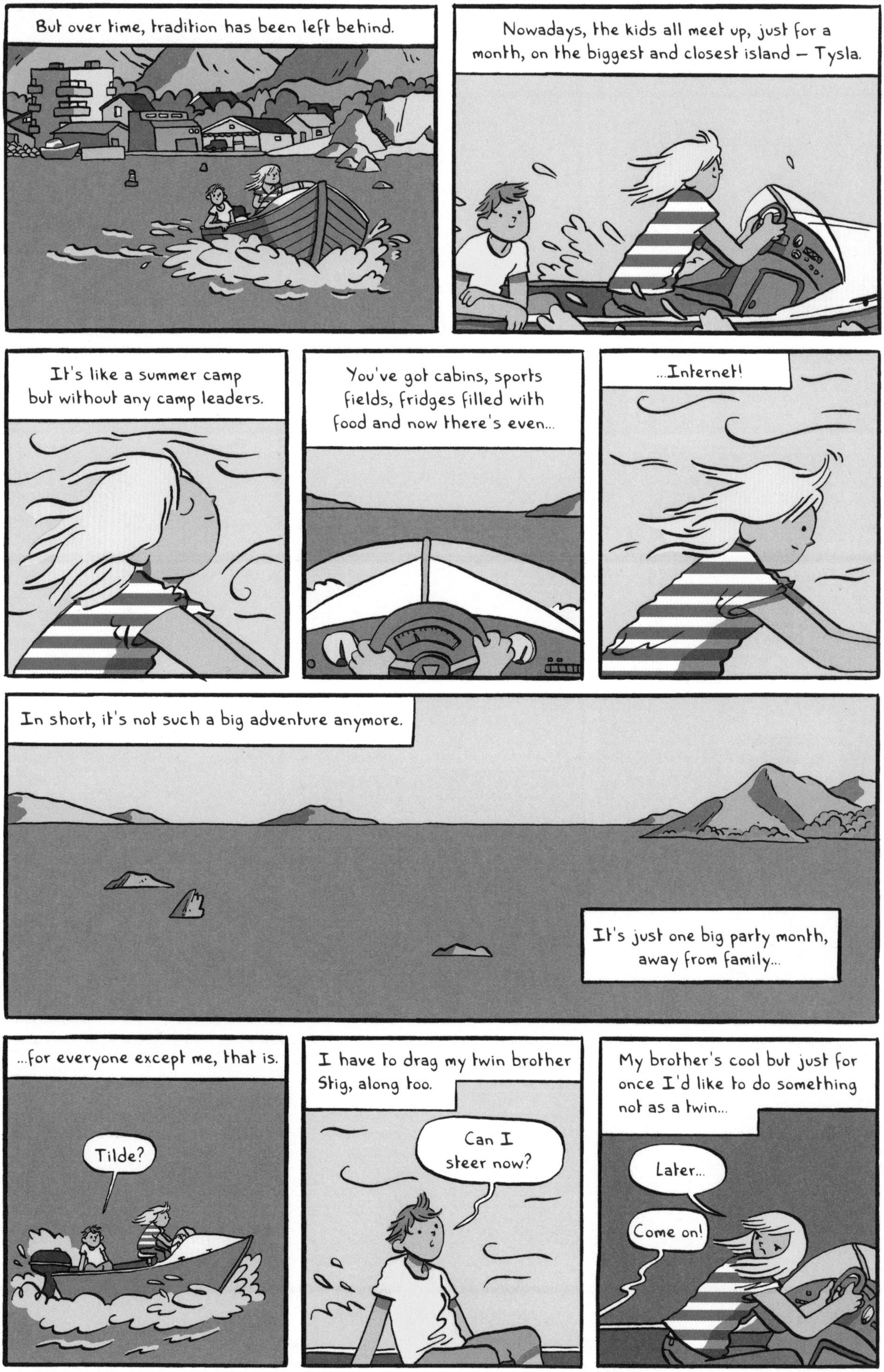

But over time, tradition has been left behind.
Nowadays, the kids all meet up, just for a month, on the biggest and closest island – Tysla.
It's like a summer camp but without any camp leaders.
You've got cabins, sports fields, fridges filled with food and now there's even...
...Internet!
In short, it's not such a big adventure anymore.
It's just one big party month, away from family...
...for everyone except me, that is.
Tilde?
I have to drag my twin brother Stig, along too.
Can I steer now?
My brother's cool but just for once I'd like to do something not as a twin...
Later...
Come on!

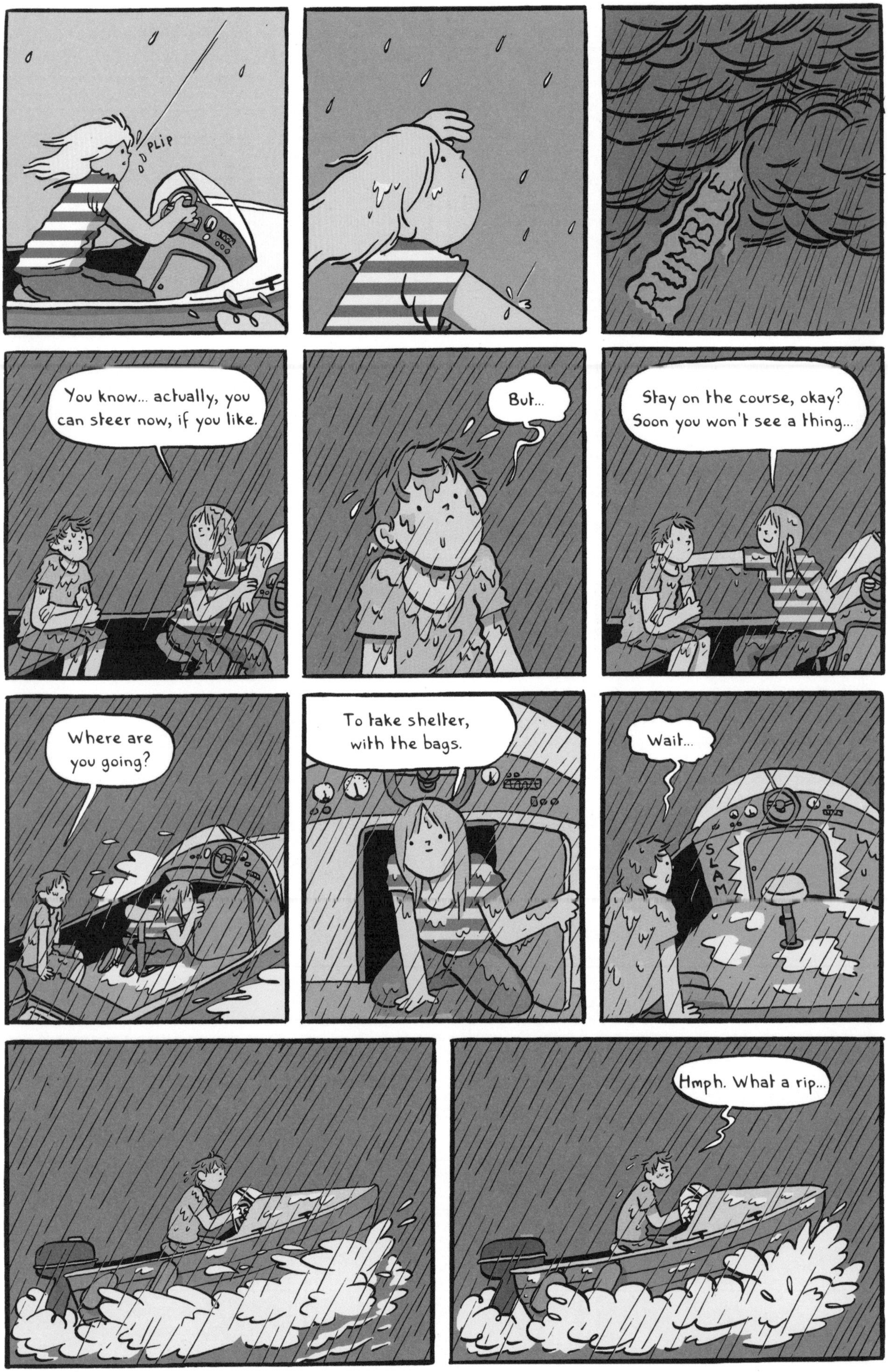
PLIP
RUMBLE
You know... actually, you can steer now, if you like.
But...
Stay on the course, okay? Soon you won't see a thing...
Where are you going?
To take shelter, with the bags.
Wait...
SLAM
Hmph. What a rip...

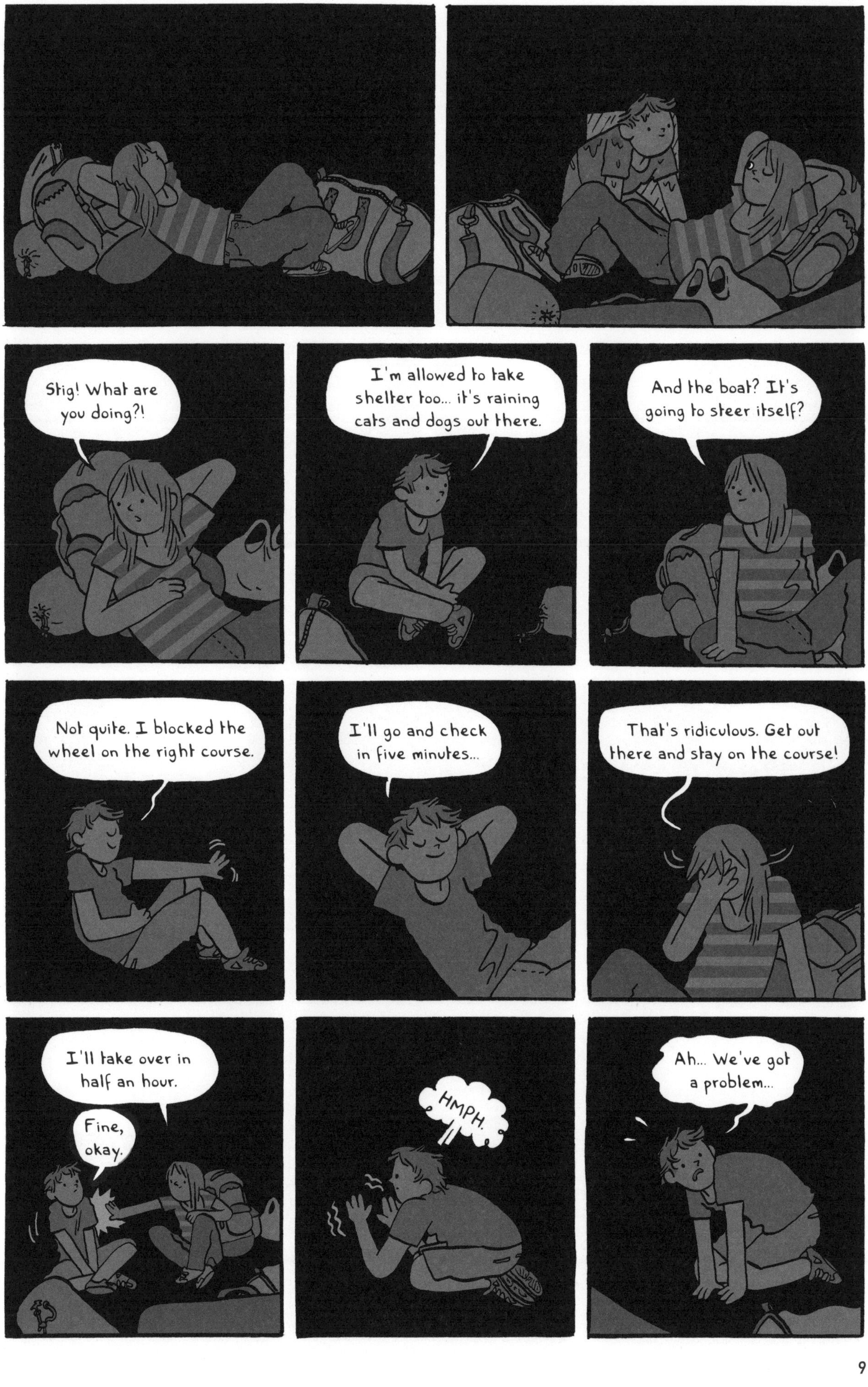

Stig! What are you doing?!
I'm allowed to take shelter too... it's raining cats and dogs out there.
And the boat? It's going to steer itself?
Not quite. I blocked the wheel on the right course.
I'll go and check in five minutes...
That's ridiculous. Get out there and stay on the course!
I'll take over in half an hour.
Fine, okay.
HMPH.
Ah... We've got a problem...

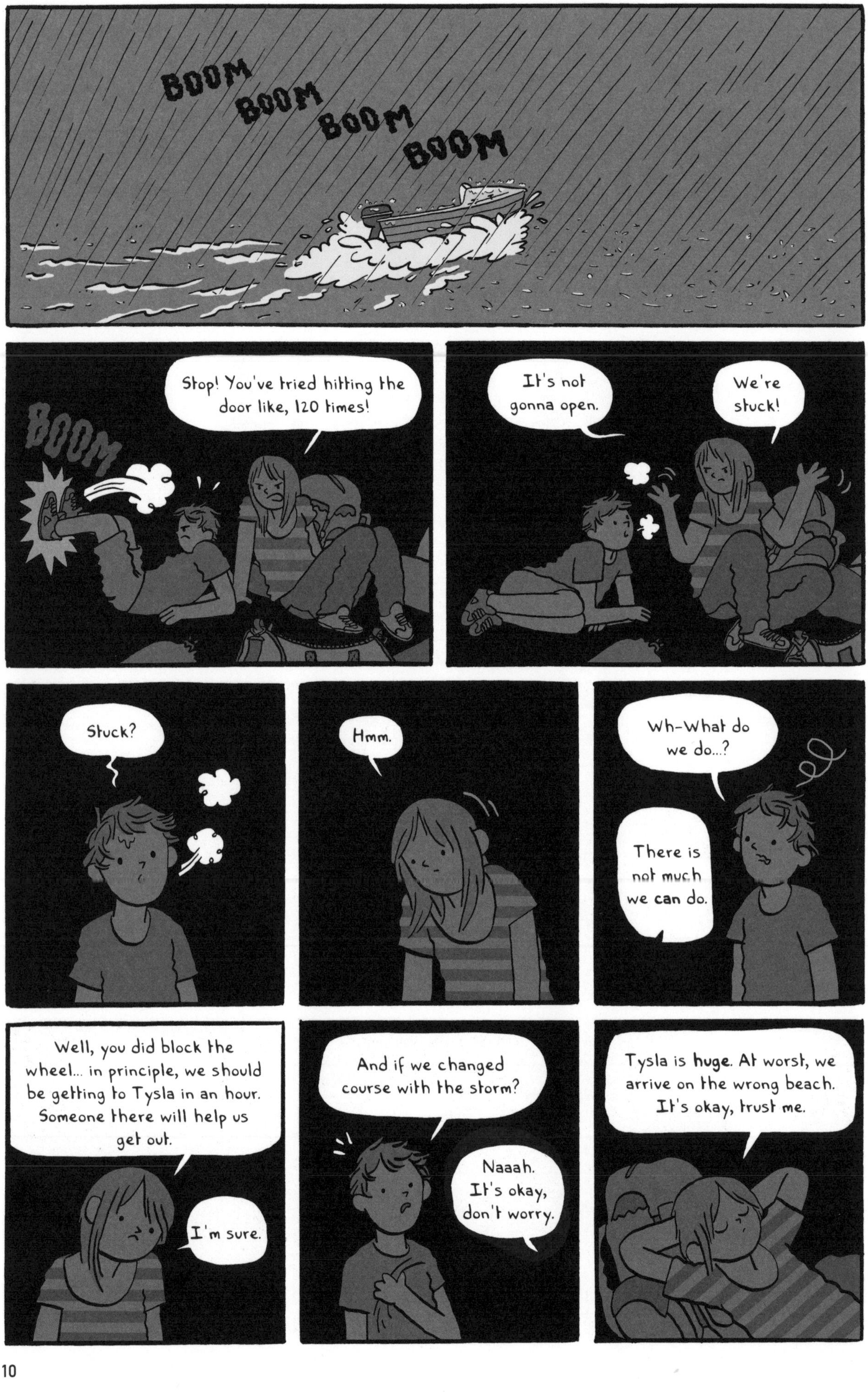
BOOM
BOOM
BOOM
BOOM
BOOM
Stop! You've tried hitting the door like, 120 times!
It's not gonna open.
We're stuck!
Stuck?
Hmm.
Wh-What do we do...?
There is not much we can do.
Well, you did block the wheel... in principle, we should be getting to Tysla in an hour. Someone there will help us get out.
I'm sure.
And if we changed course with the storm?
Naaah. It's okay, don't worry.
Tysla is huge. At worst, we arrive on the wrong beach. It's okay, trust me.

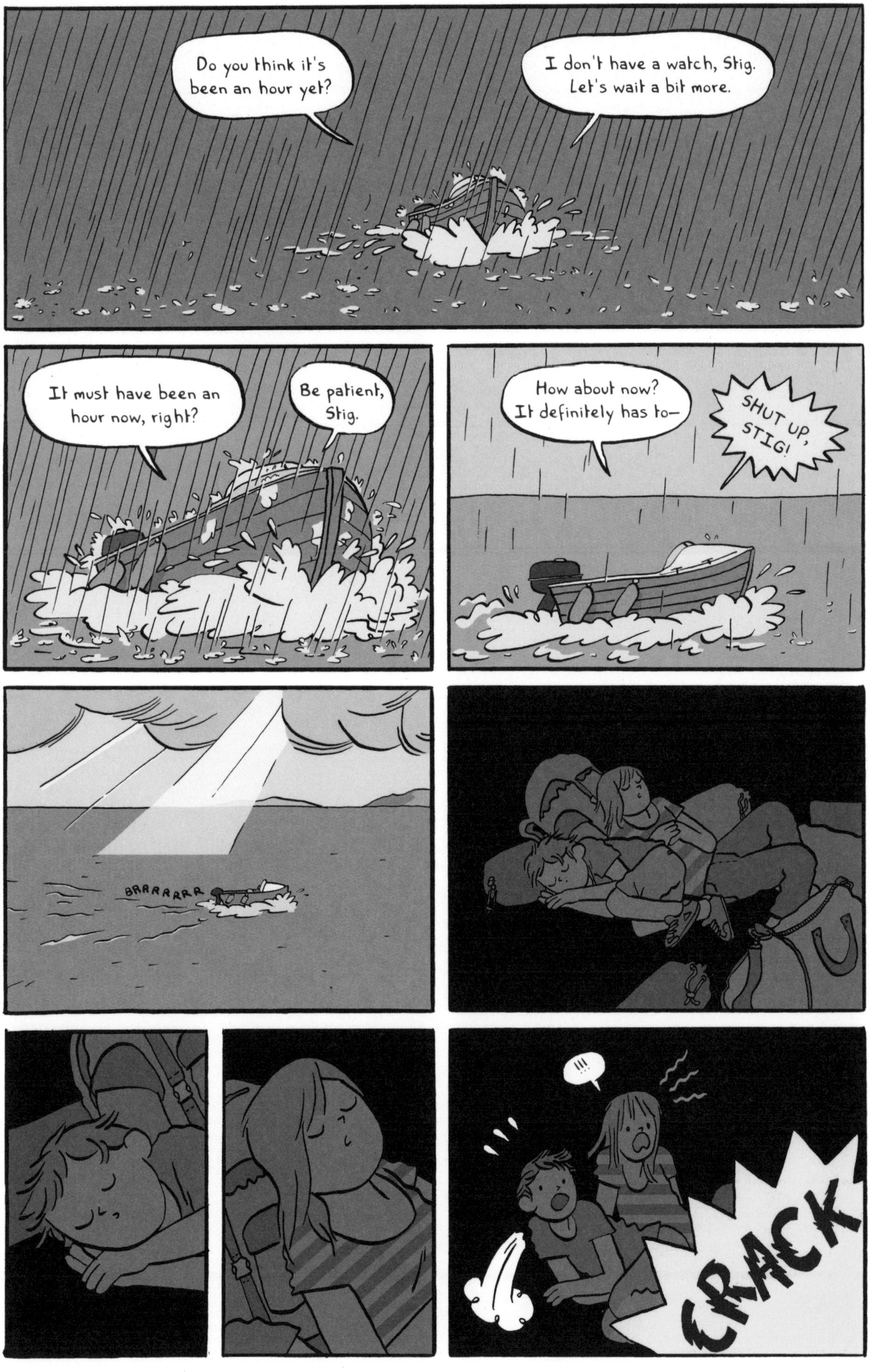
Do you think it's been an hour yet?
I don't have a watch, Stig. Let's wait a bit more.
It must have been an hour now, right?
Be patient, Stig.
How about now? It definitely has to—
SHUT UP, STIG!
BRRRRRRR
!!!
CRACK

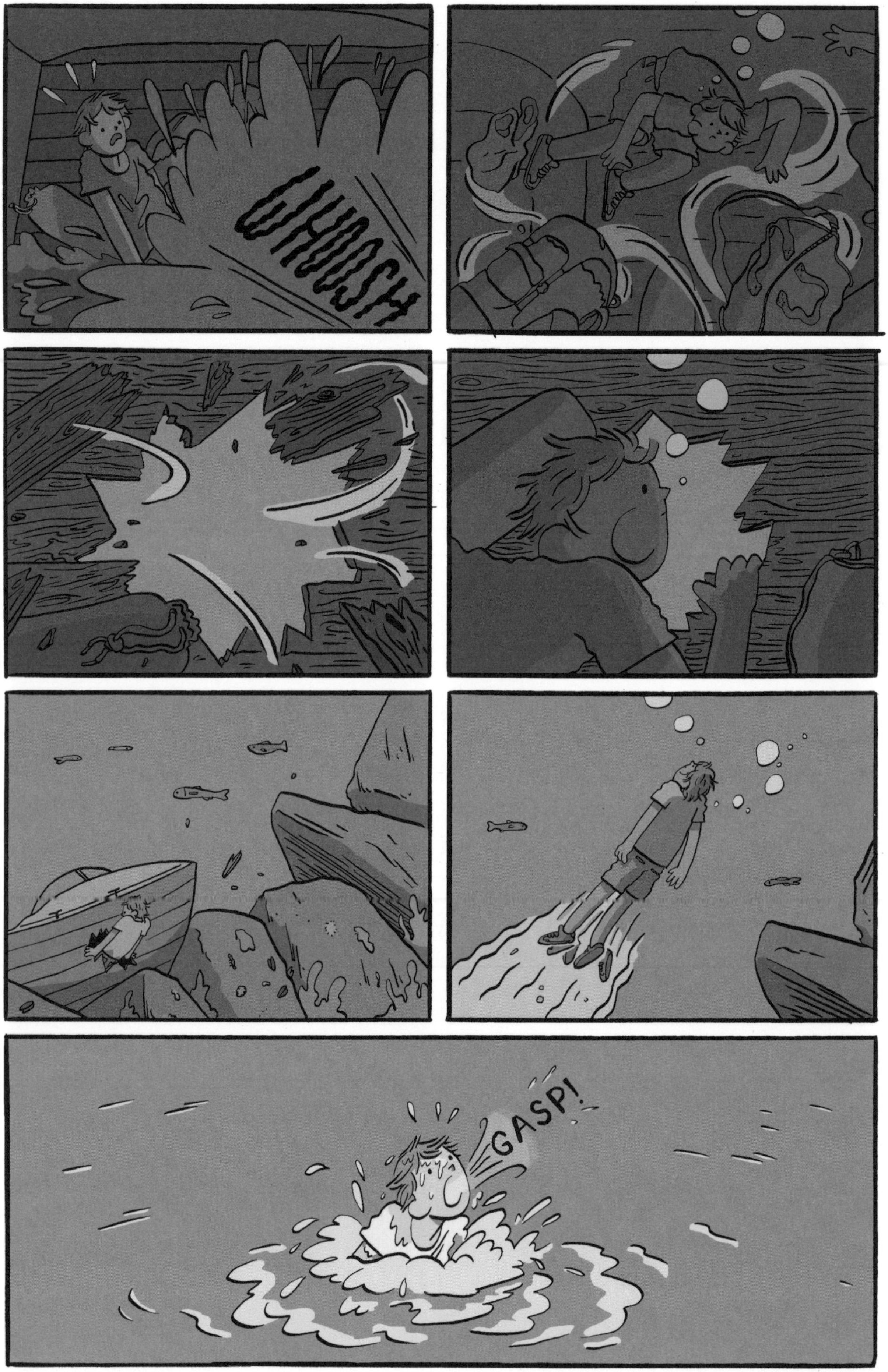
WHOOSH
GASP!

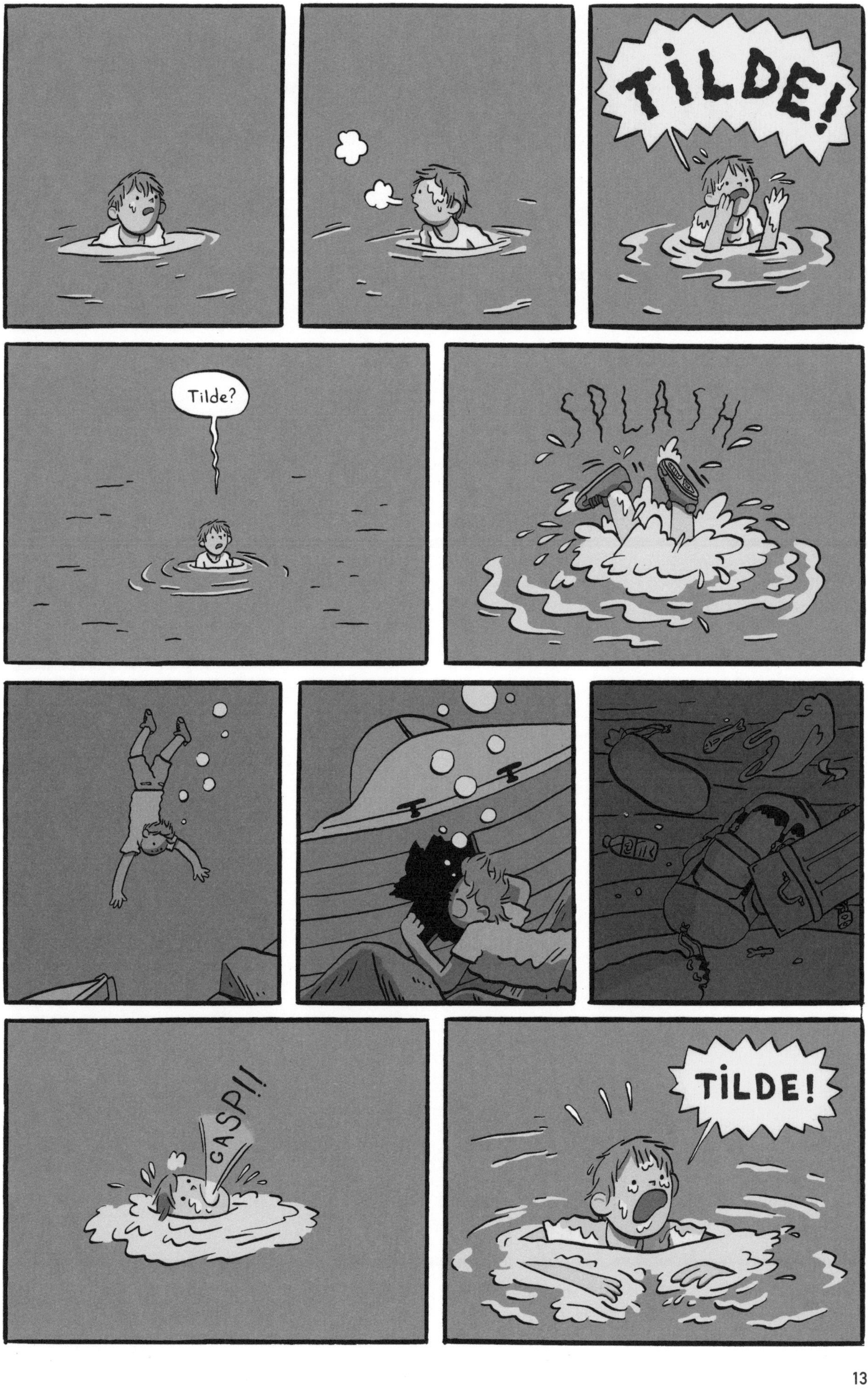
TILDE!
Tilde?
SPLASH
GASP!!
TILDE!

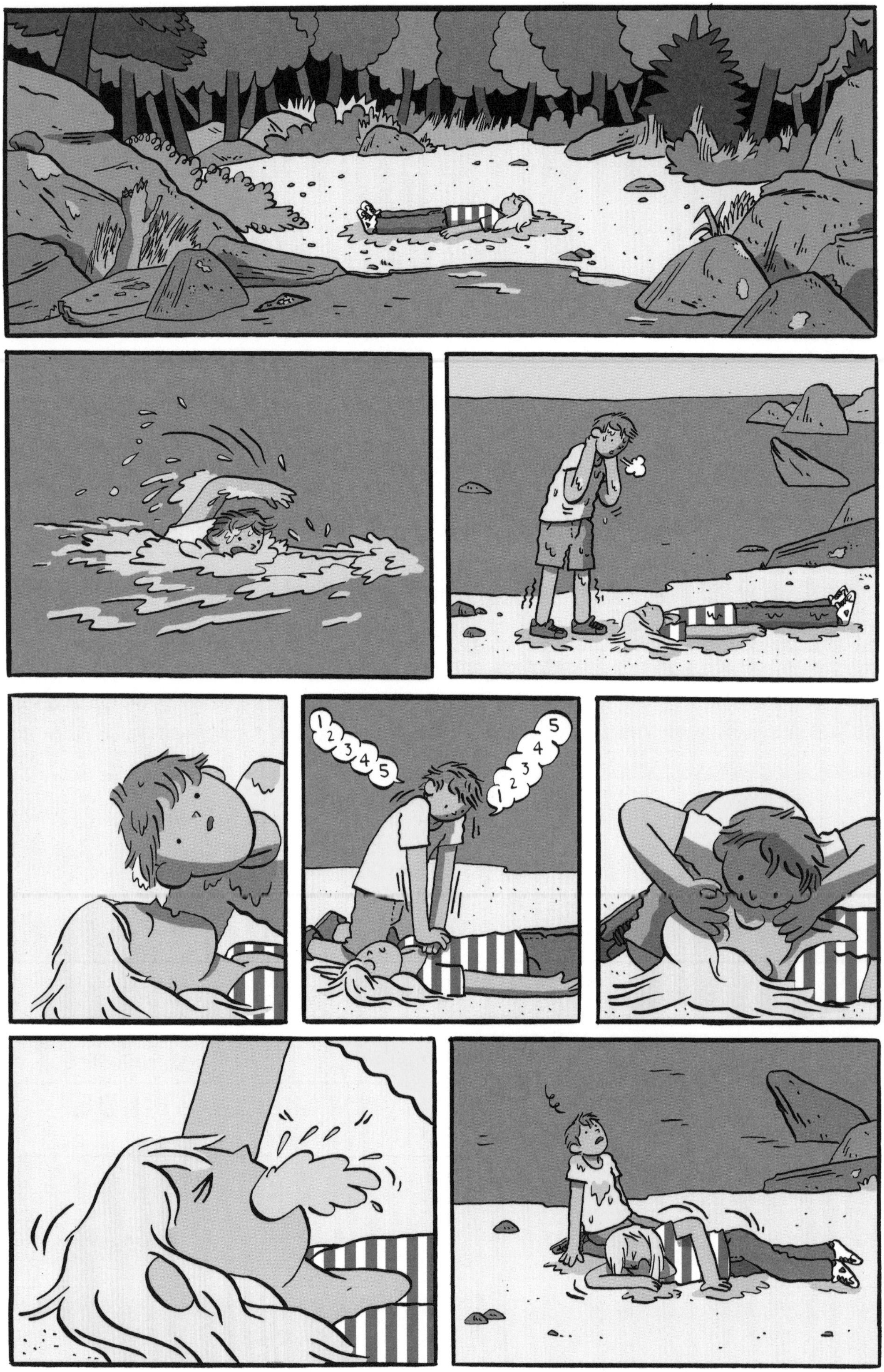
1 2 3 4 5
1 2 3 4 5

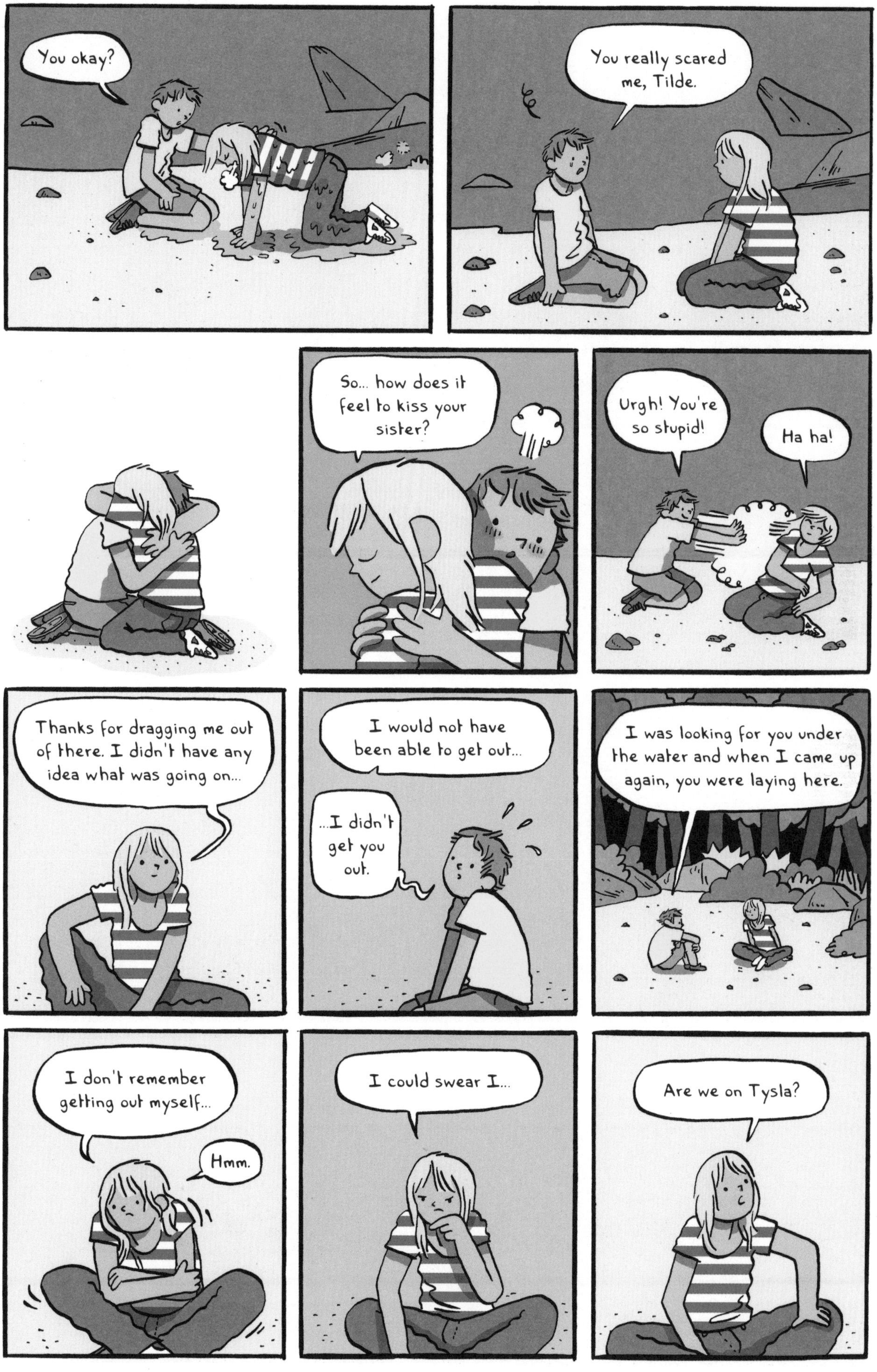
You okay?
You really scared me, Tilde.
So... how does it feel to kiss your sister?
Urgh! You're so stupid!
Ha ha!
Thanks for dragging me out of there. I didn't have any idea what was going on...
I would not have been able to get out...
...I didn't get you out.
I was looking for you under the water and when I came up again, you were laying here.
I don't remember getting out myself...
Hmm.
I could swear I...
Are we on Tysla?

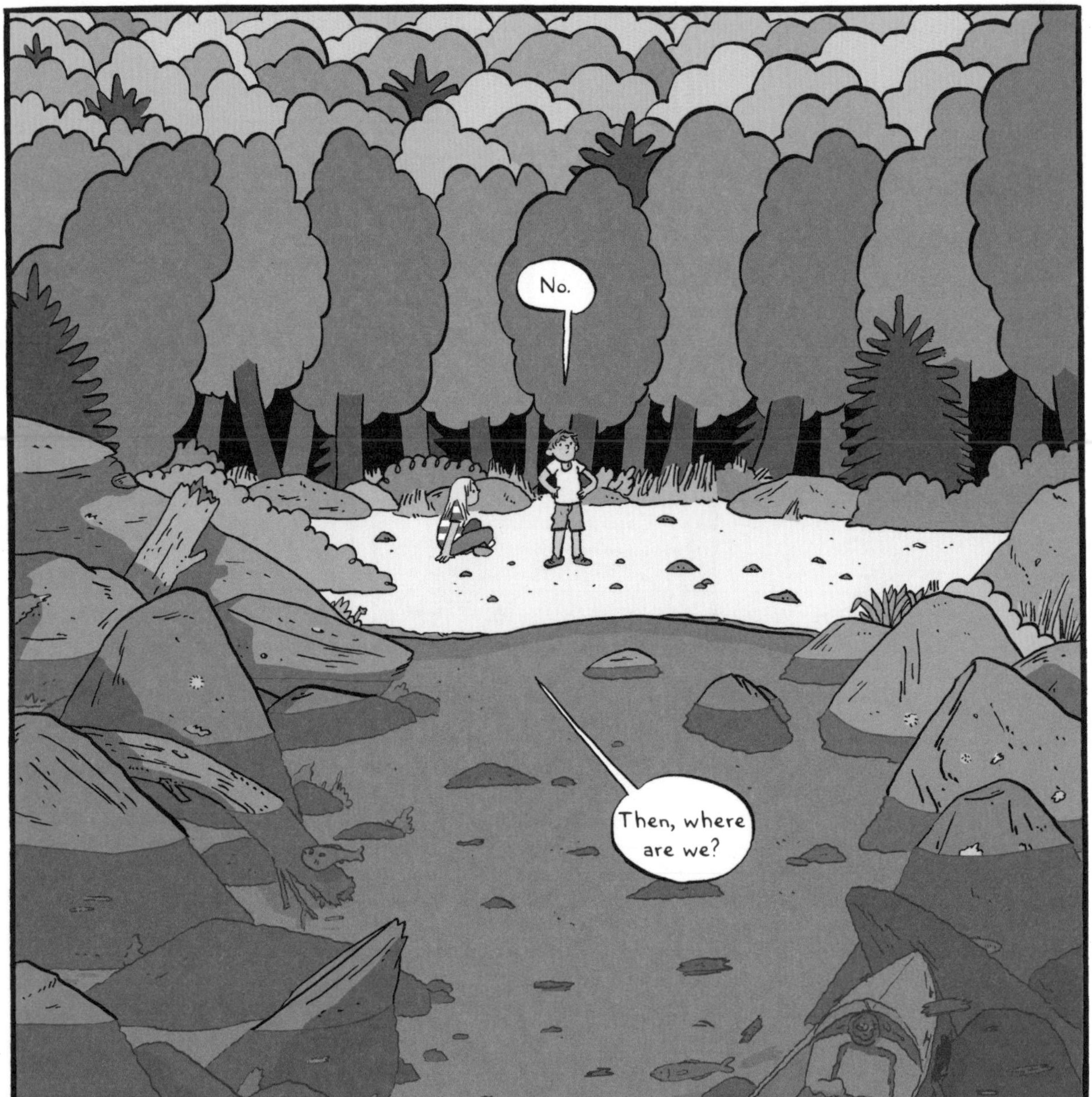
No.
Then, where are we?

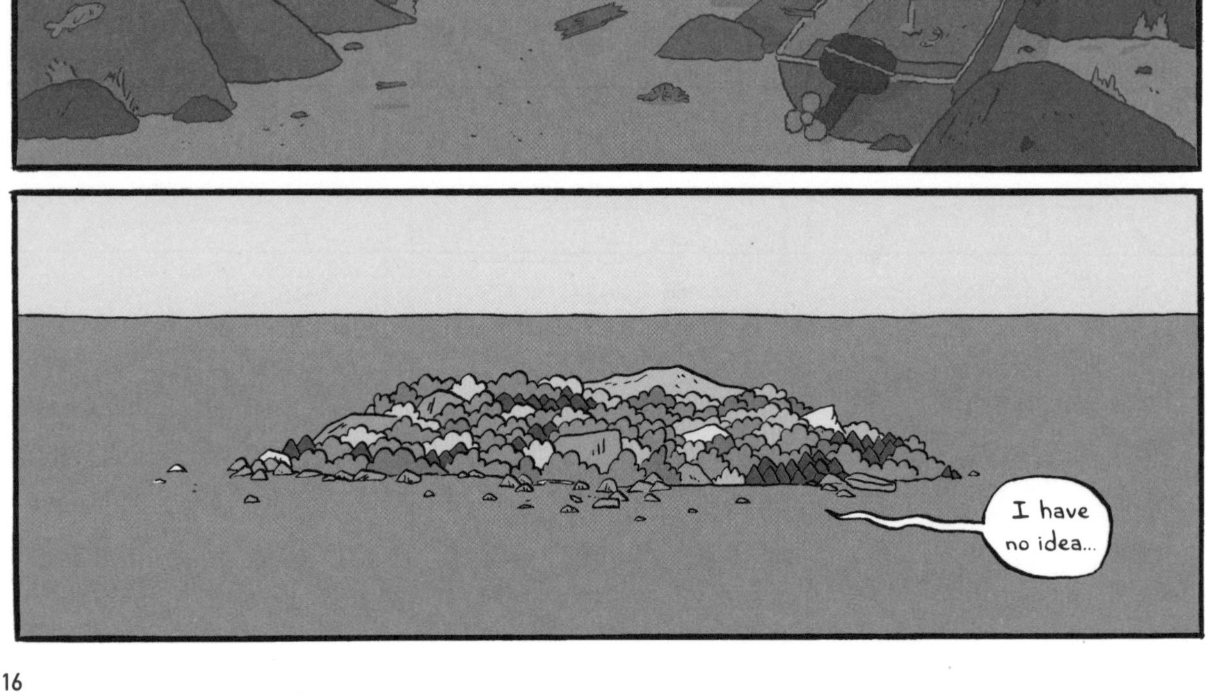
I have no idea...

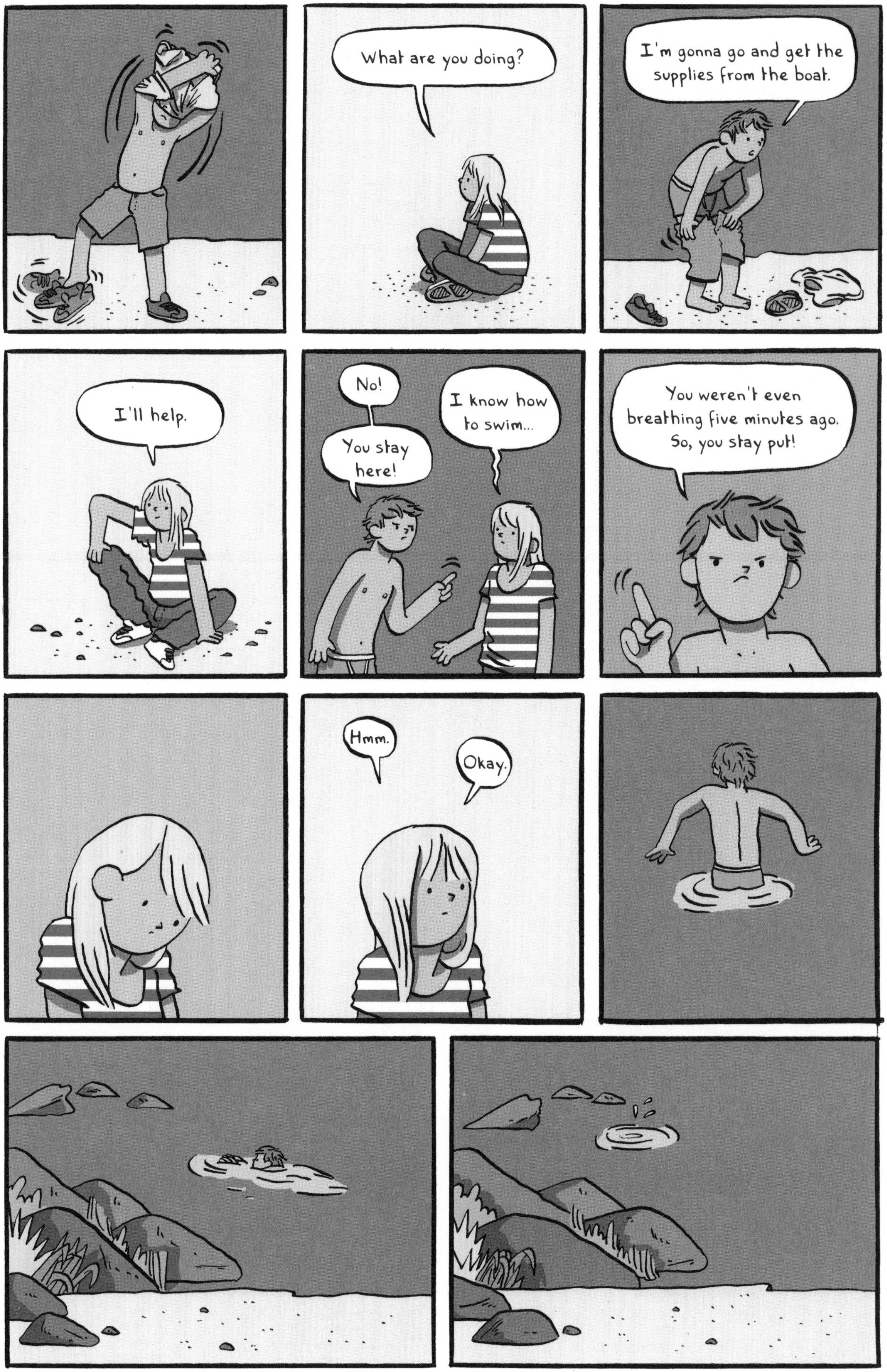
What are you doing?
I'm gonna go and get the supplies from the boat.
I'll help.
No!
You stay here!
I know how to swim...
You weren't even breathing five minutes ago. So, you stay put!
Hmm.
Okay.

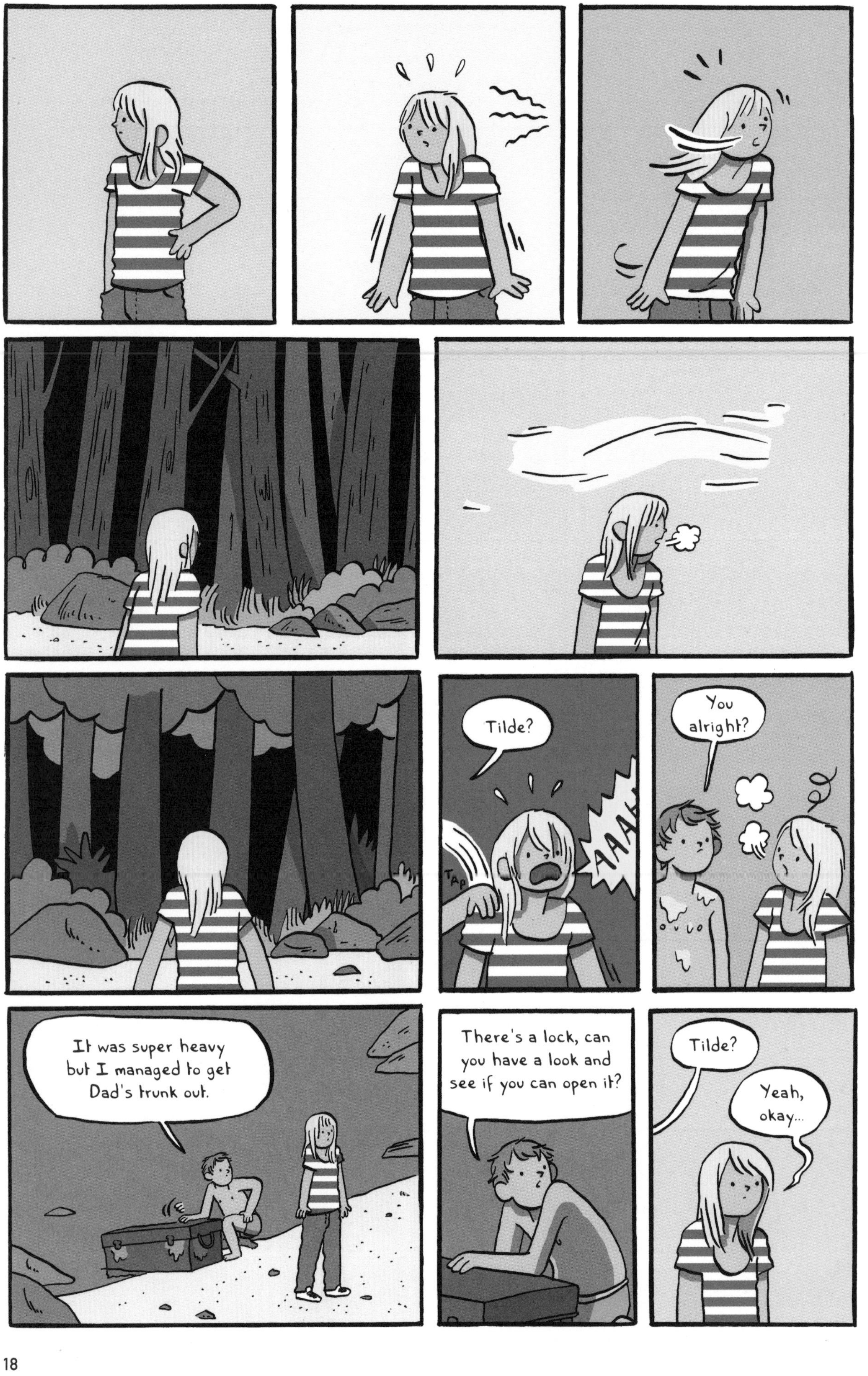
Tilde?
TAP
AAAA
You alright?
It was super heavy but I managed to get Dad's trunk out.
There's a lock, can you have a look and see if you can open it?
Tilde?
Yeah, okay...

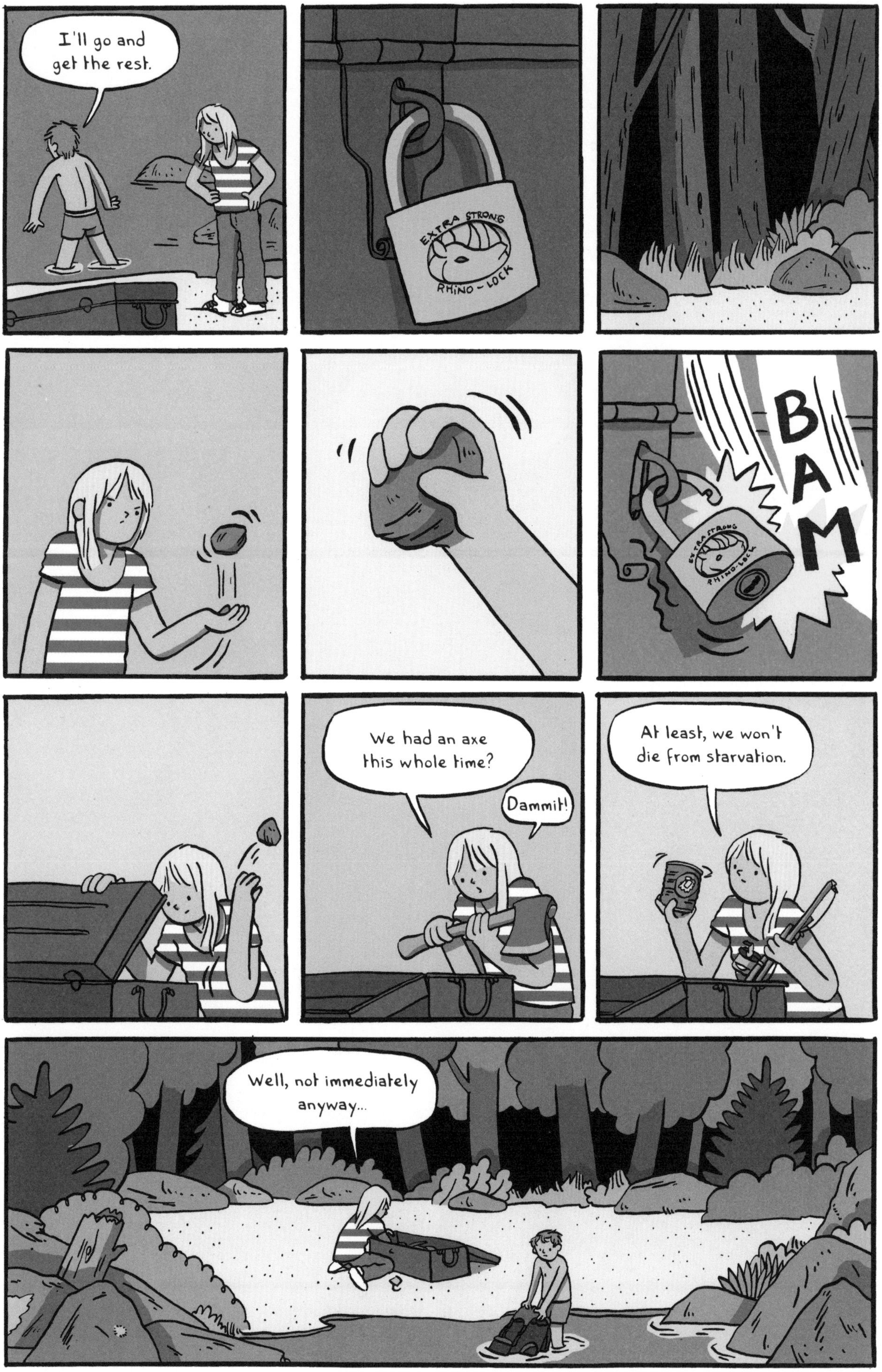
I'll go and get the rest.
EXTRA STRONG RHINO-LOCK
BAM
We had an axe this whole time?
Dammit!
At least, we won't die from starvation.
Well, not immediately anyway...

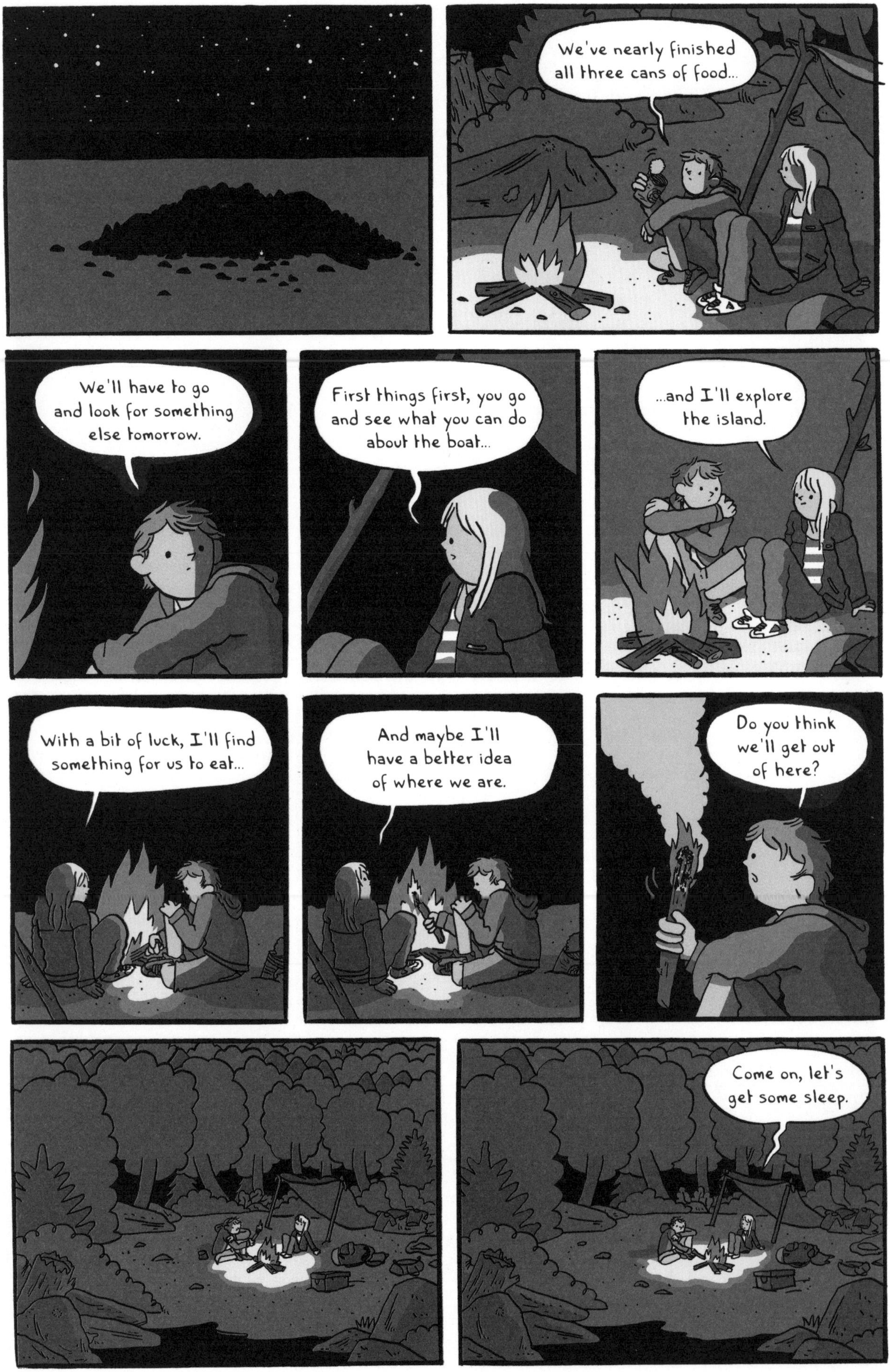
We've nearly finished all three cans of food...
We'll have to go and look for something else tomorrow.
First things first, you go and see what you can do about the boat...
...and I'll explore the island.
With a bit of luck, I'll find something for us to eat...
And maybe I'll have a better idea of where we are.
Do you think we'll get out of here?
Come on, let's get some sleep.

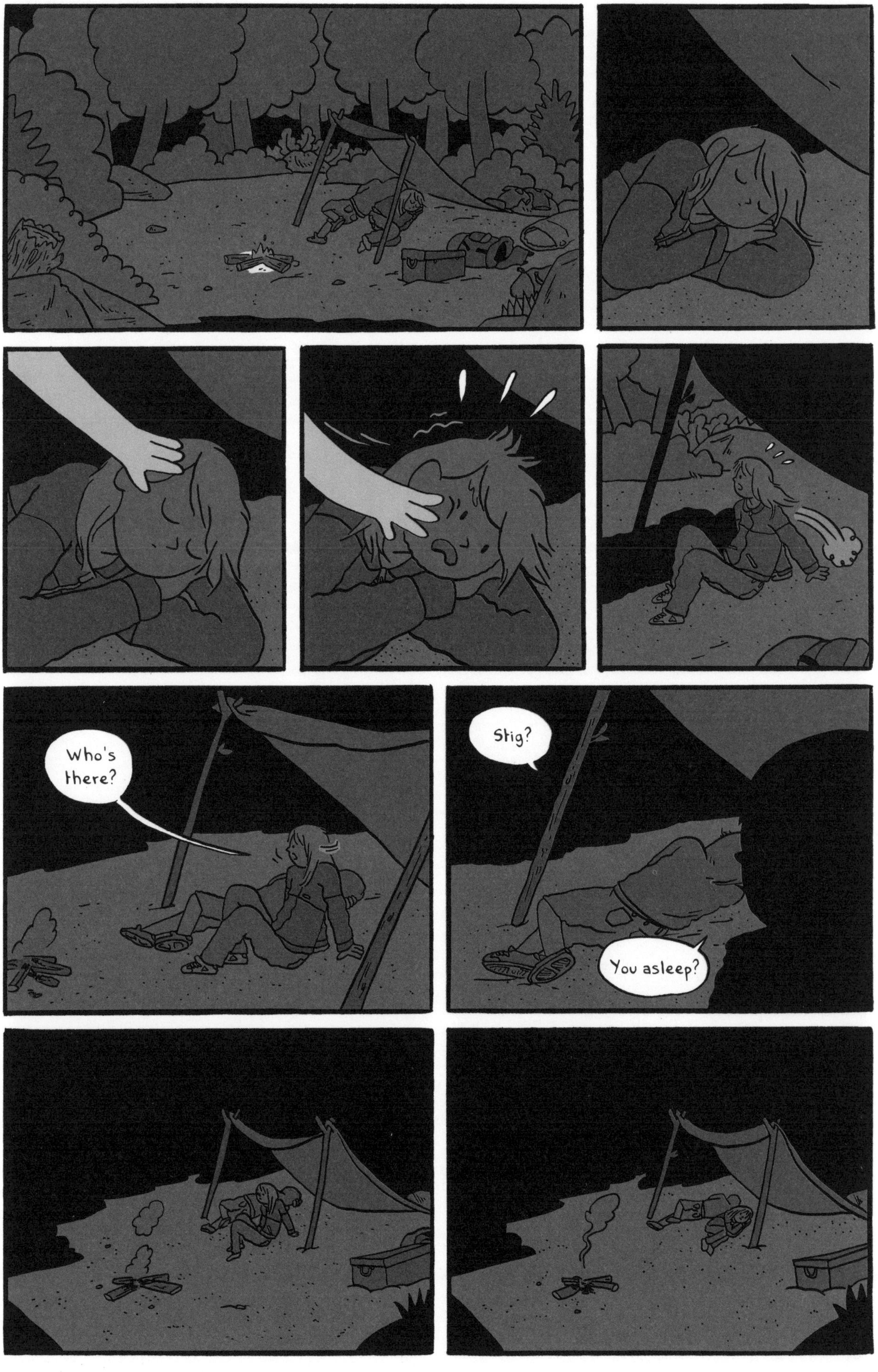
Who's there?
Stig?
You asleep?

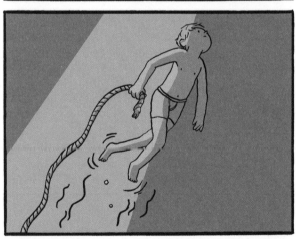

How's it going?

Yeah, fine! Don't worry about me.

Okay, I'm going to walk around.

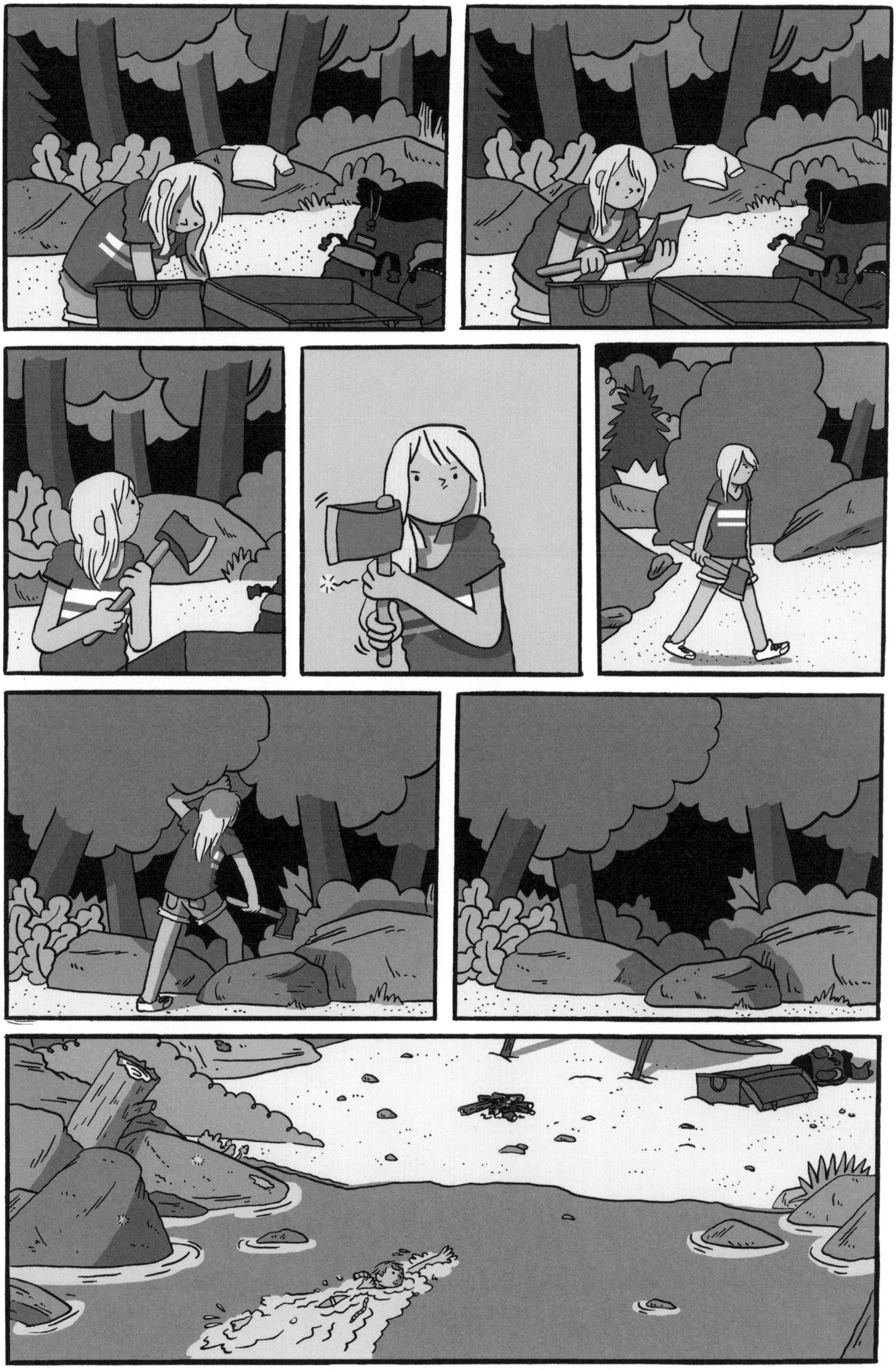

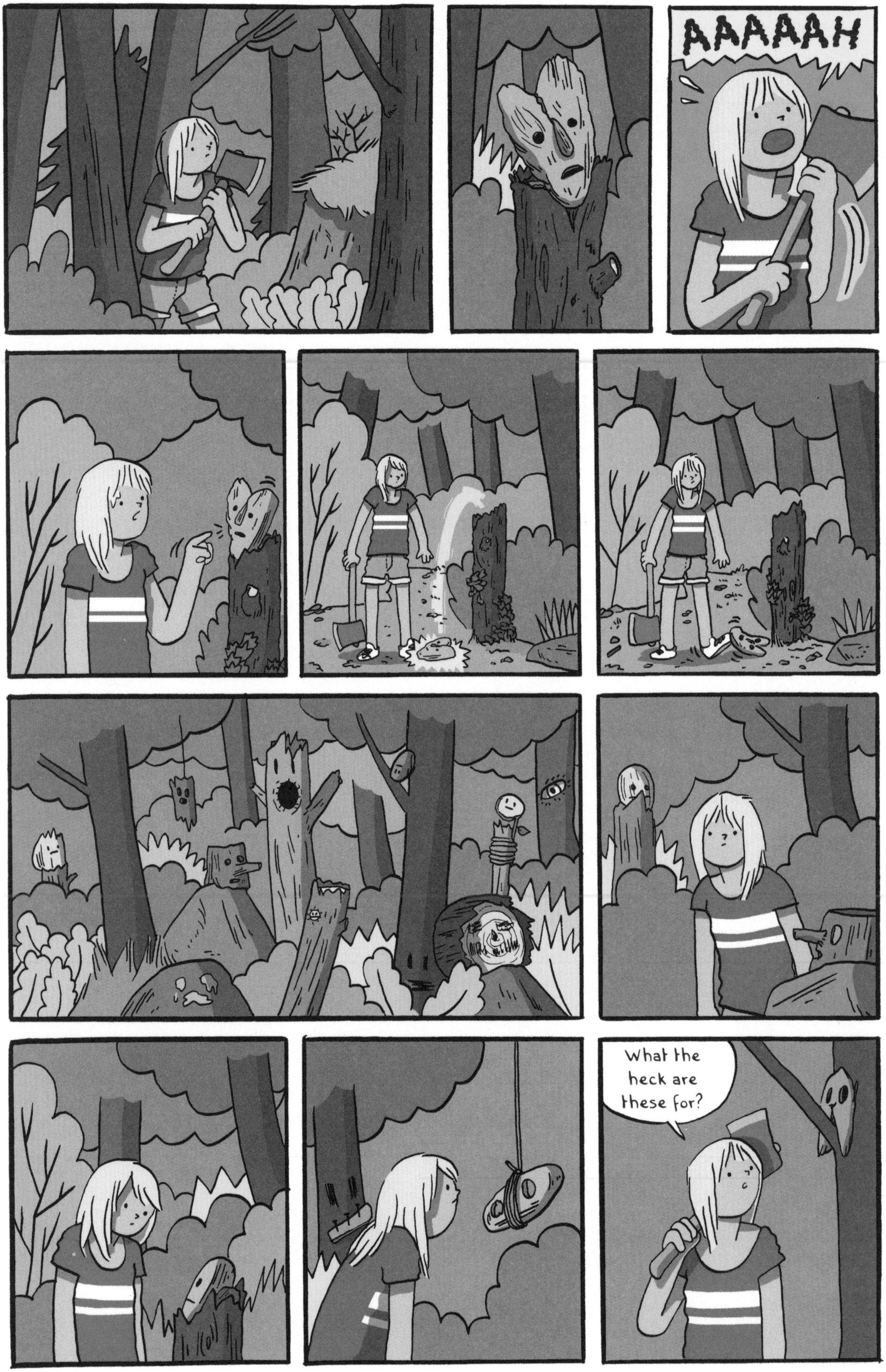
AAAAAH
What the heck are these for?

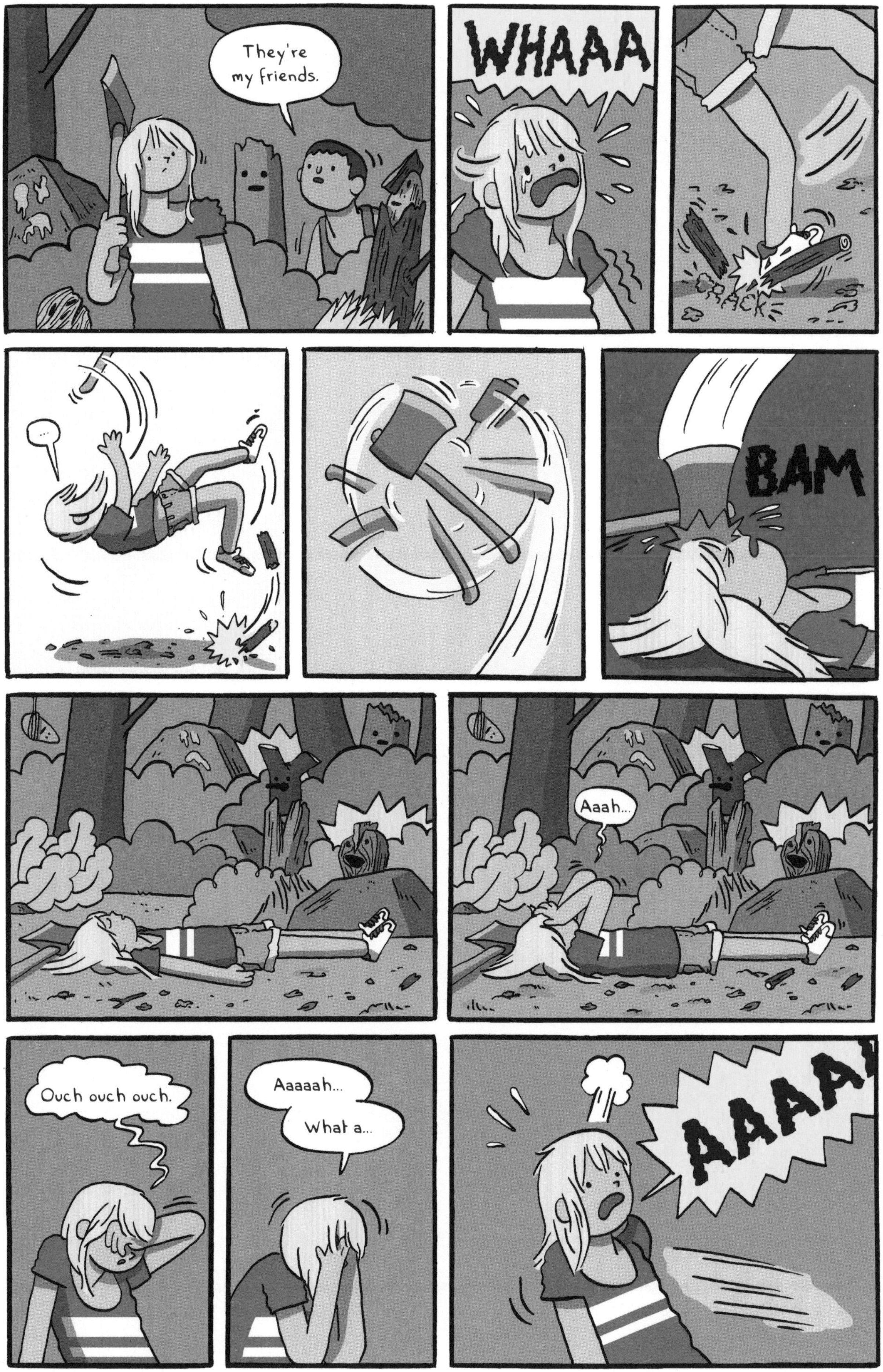
They're my friends.
WHAAA
CRACK
...
BAM
Aaah...
Ouch ouch ouch.
Aaaaah...
What a...
AAAA

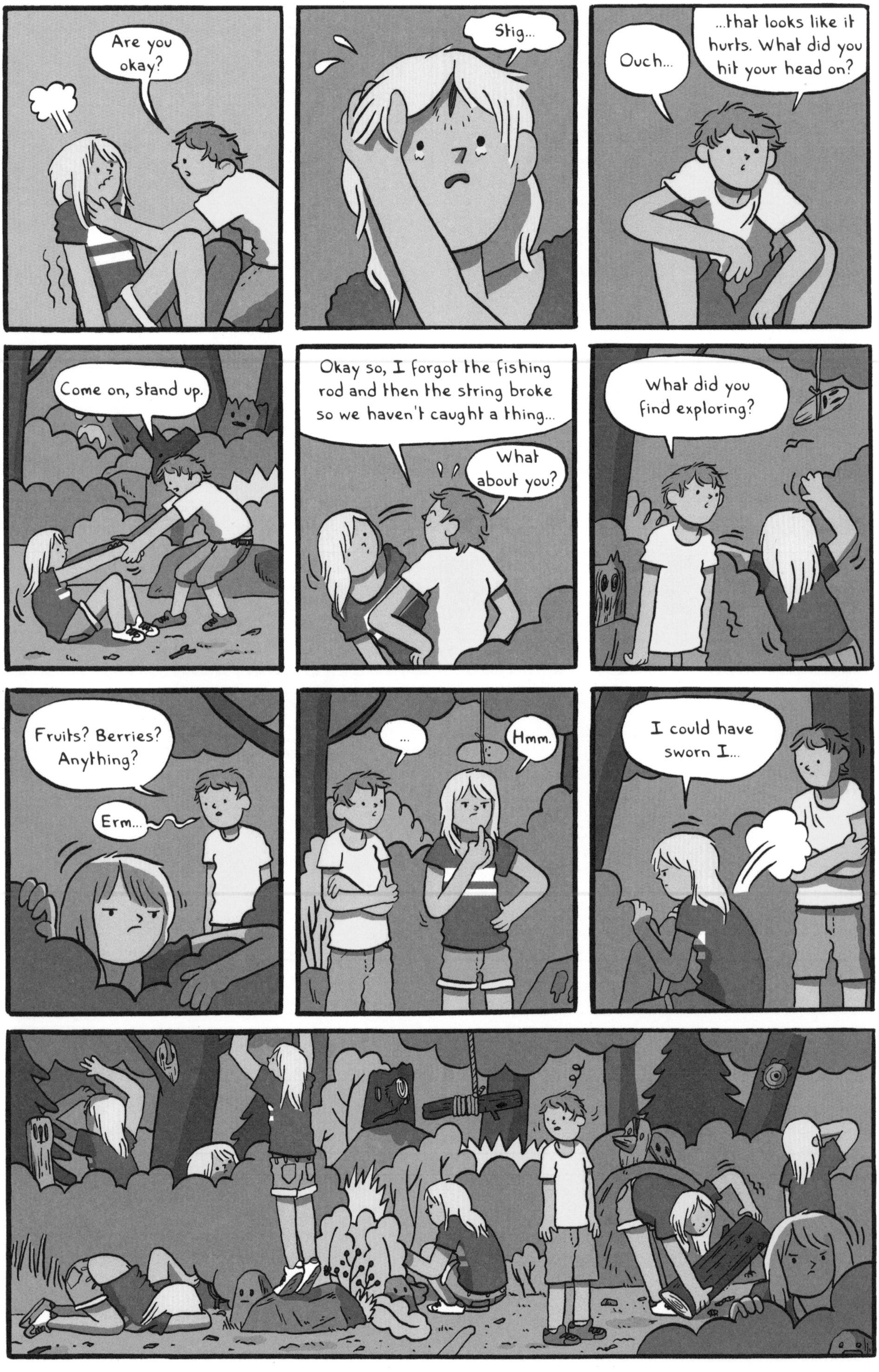
Are you okay?
Stig...
Ouch...
...that looks like it hurts. What did you hit your head on?
Come on, stand up.
Okay so, I forgot the fishing rod and then the string broke so we haven't caught a thing...
What about you?
What did you find exploring?
Fruits? Berries? Anything?
Erm...
...
Hmm.
I could have sworn I...

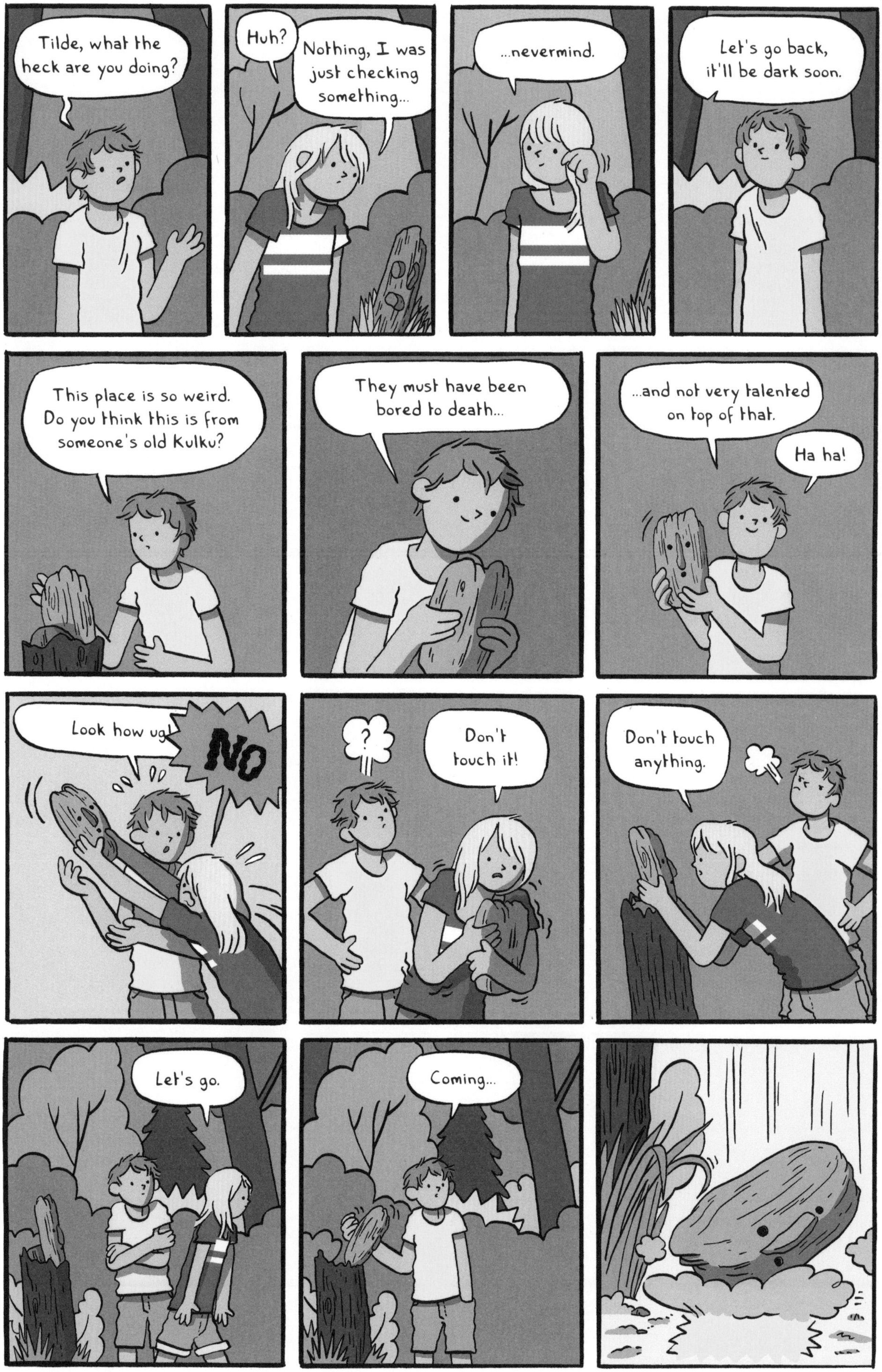
Tilde, what the heck are you doing?
Huh?
Nothing, I was just checking something...
...nevermind.
Let's go back, it'll be dark soon.
This place is so weird. Do you think this is from someone's old Kulku?
They must have been bored to death...
...and not very talented on top of that.
Ha ha!
Look how ug!
NO
?
Don't touch it!
Don't touch anything.
Let's go.
Coming...

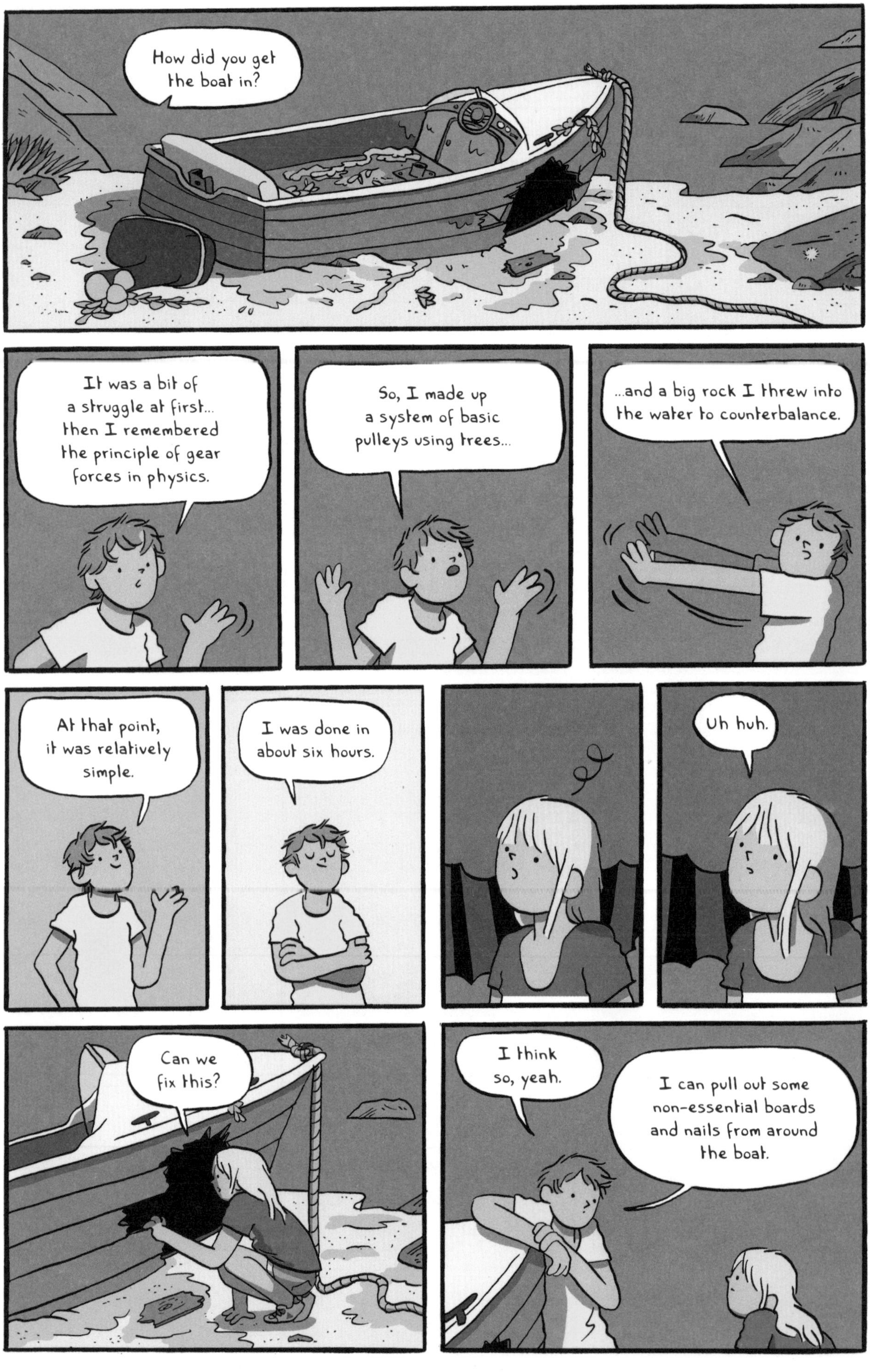
How did you get the boat in?
It was a bit of a struggle at first... then I remembered the principle of gear forces in physics.
So, I made up a system of basic pulleys using trees...
...and a big rock I threw into the water to counterbalance.
At that point, it was relatively simple.
I was done in about six hours.
Uh huh.
Can we fix this?
I think so, yeah.
I can pull out some non-essential boards and nails from around the boat.

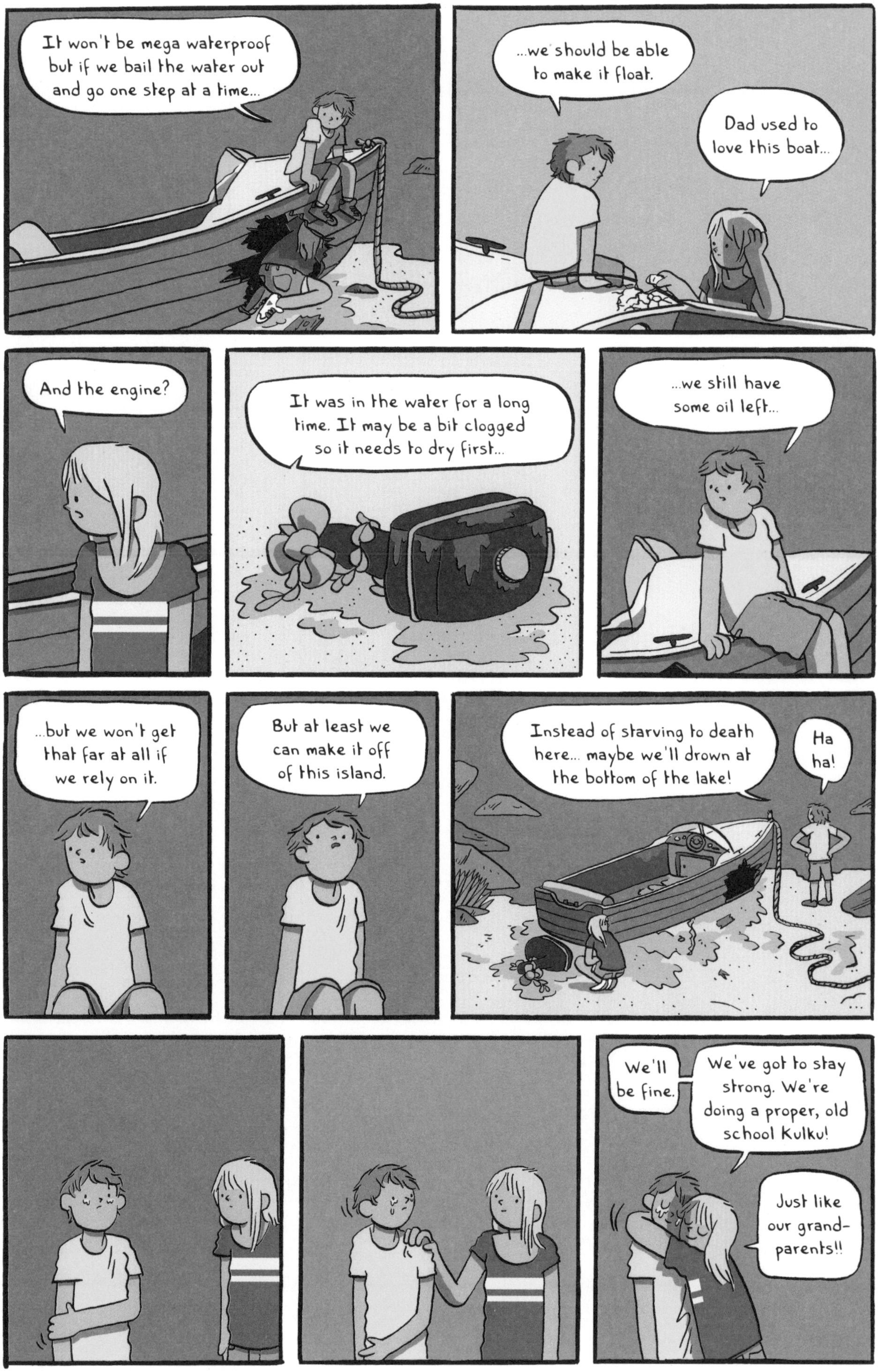
It won't be mega waterproof but if we bail the water out and go one step at a time...
...we should be able to make it float.
Dad used to love this boat...
And the engine?
It was in the water for a long time. It may be a bit clogged so it needs to dry first...
...we still have some oil left...
...but we won't get that far at all if we rely on it.
But at least we can make it off of this island.
Instead of starving to death here... maybe we'll drown at the bottom of the lake!
Ha ha!
We'll be fine.
We've got to stay strong. We're doing a proper, old school Kulku!
Just like our grand-parents!!

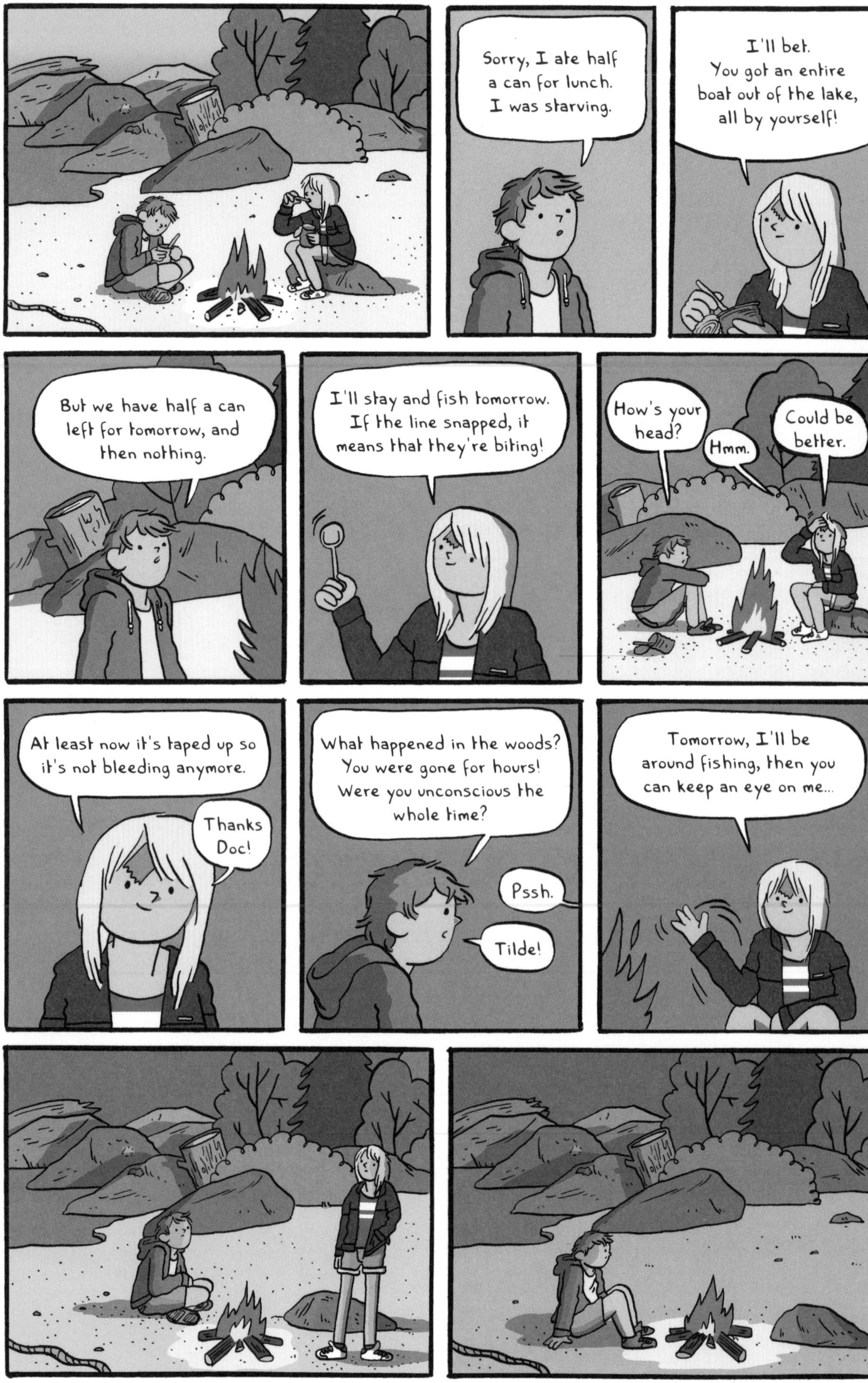
Sorry, I ate half a can for lunch. I was starving.
I'll bet. You got an entire boat out of the lake, all by yourself!
But we have half a can left for tomorrow, and then nothing.
I'll stay and fish tomorrow. If the line snapped, it means that they're biting!
How's your head?
Hmm.
Could be better.
At least now it's taped up so it's not bleeding anymore.
Thanks Doc!
What happened in the woods? You were gone for hours! Were you unconscious the whole time?
Pssh.
Tilde!
Tomorrow, I'll be around fishing, then you can keep an eye on me...

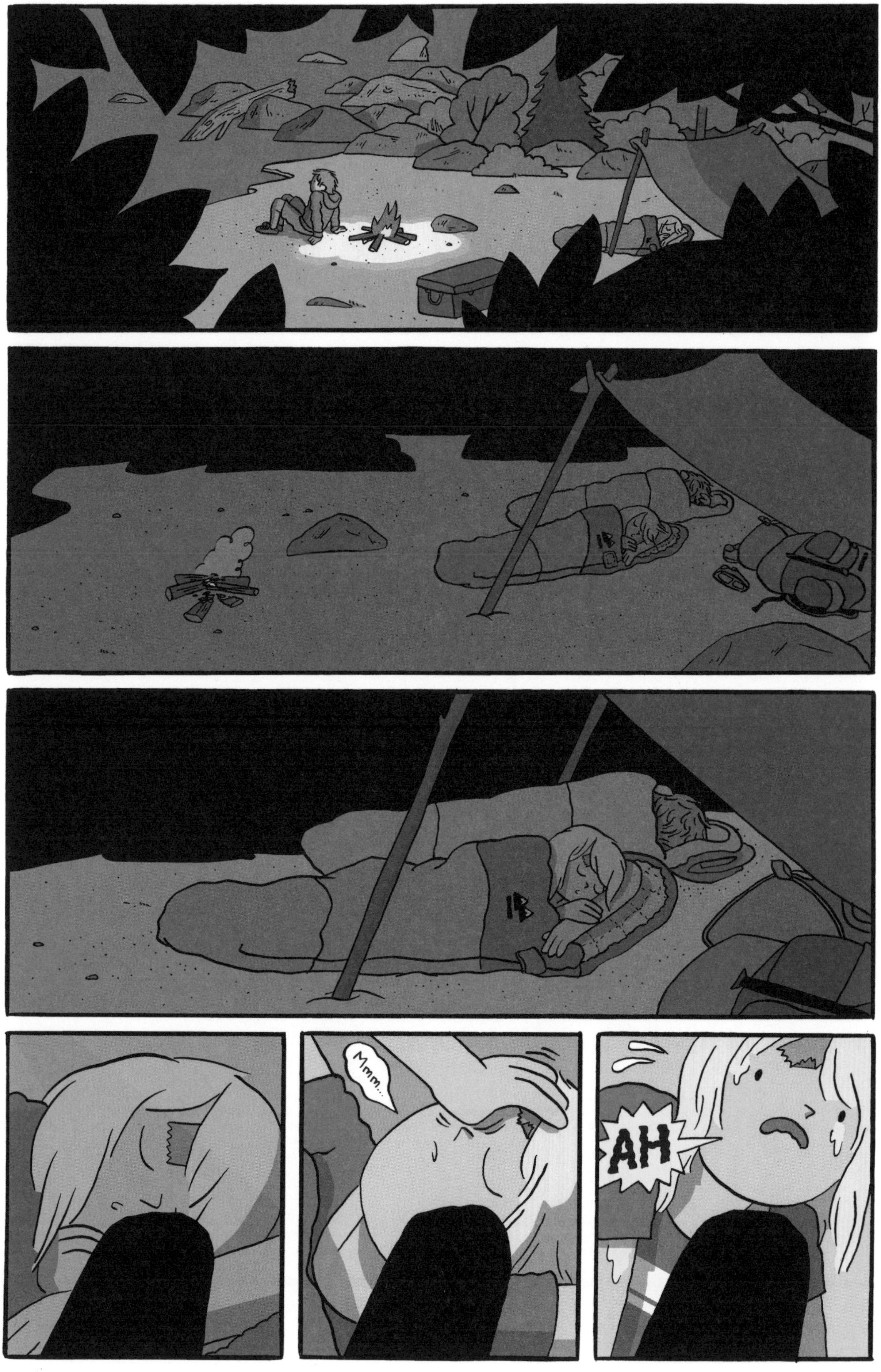
Mmm...
AH

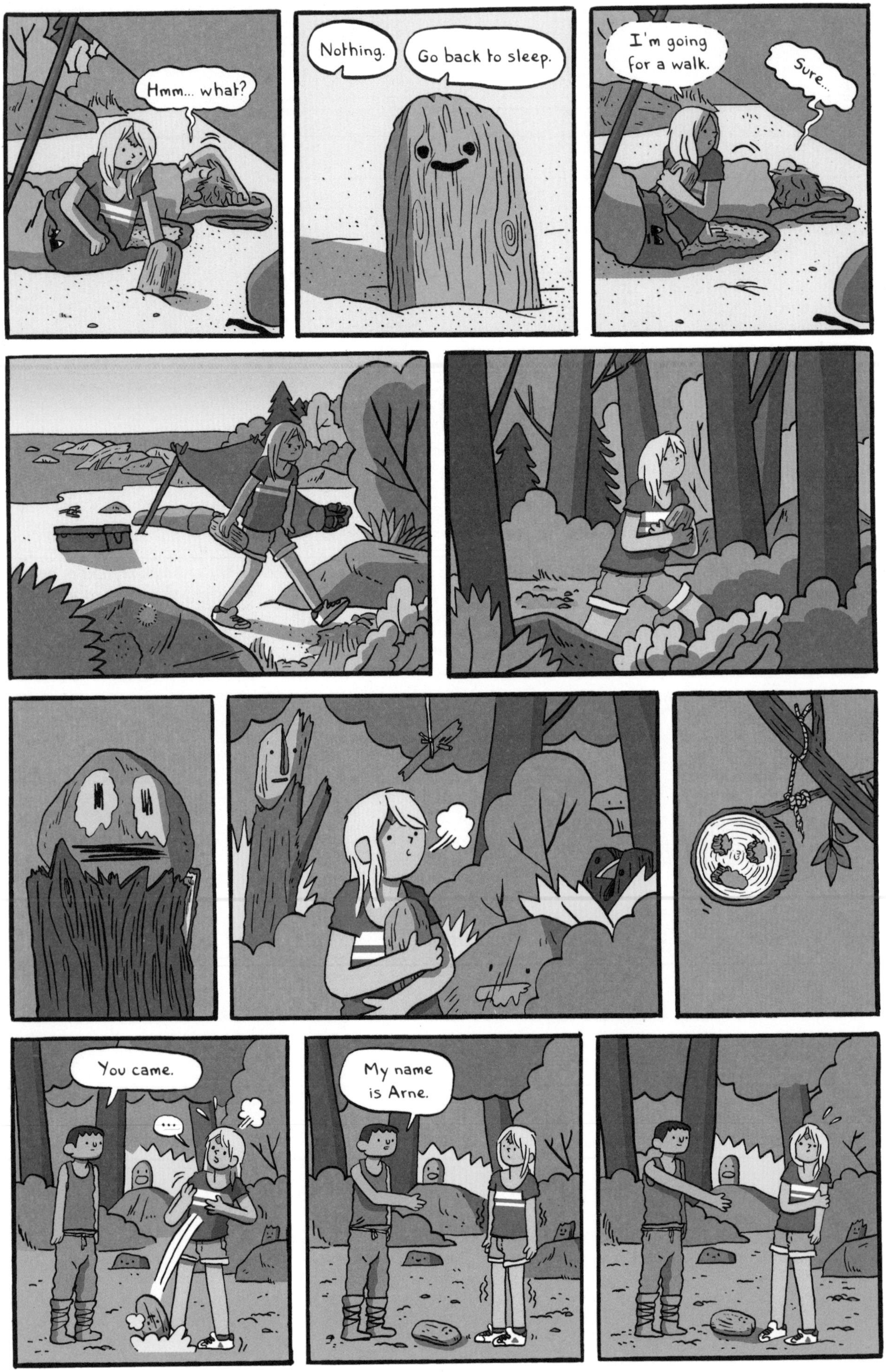
Hmm... what?
Nothing.
Go back to sleep.
I'm going for a walk.
Sure...
You came.
...
My name is Arne.

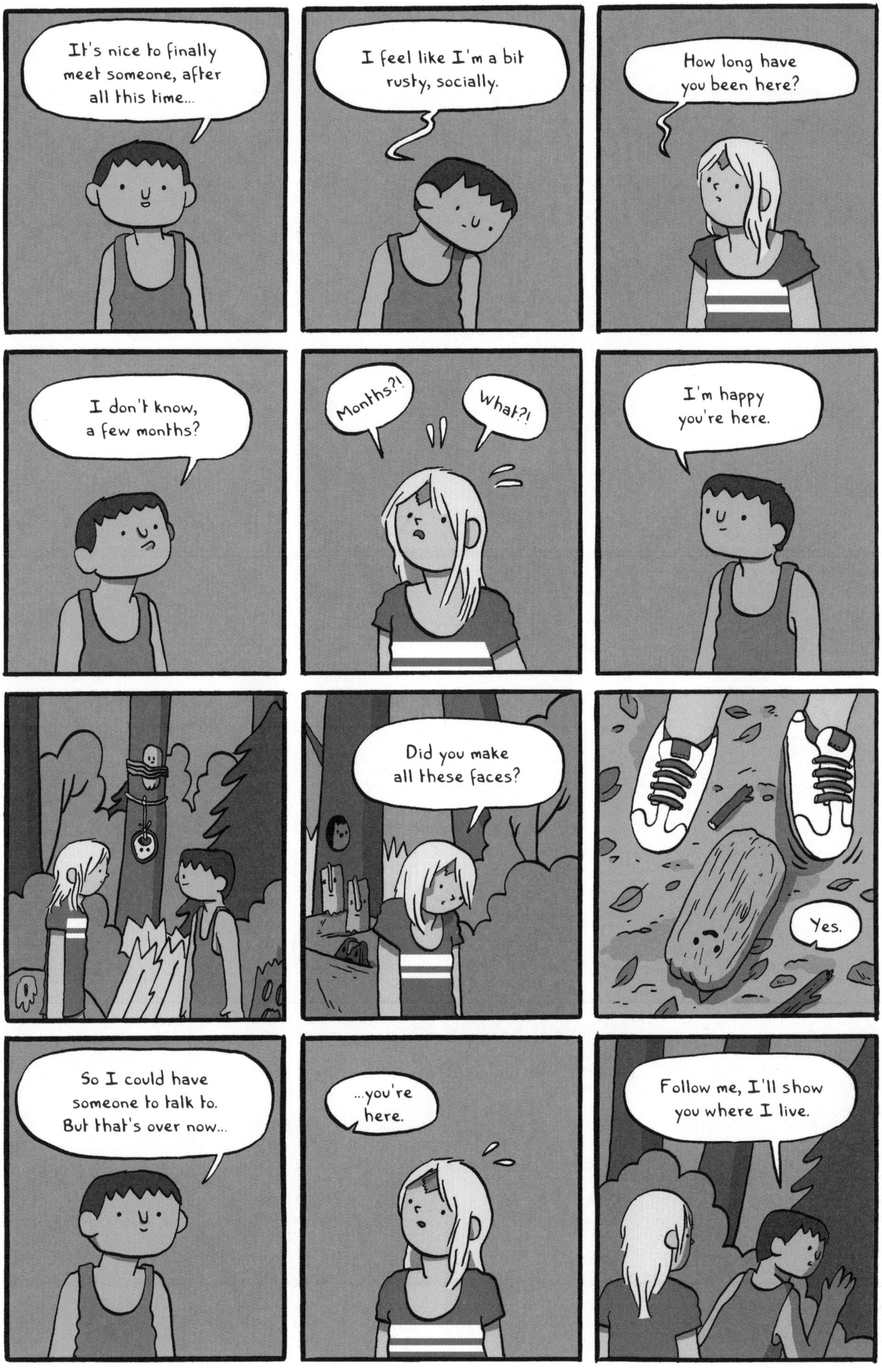
It's nice to finally meet someone, after all this time...
I feel like I'm a bit rusty, socially.
How long have you been here?
I don't know, a few months?
Months?!
What?!
I'm happy you're here.
Did you make all these faces?
Yes.
So I could have someone to talk to. But that's over now...
...you're here.
Follow me, I'll show you where I live.

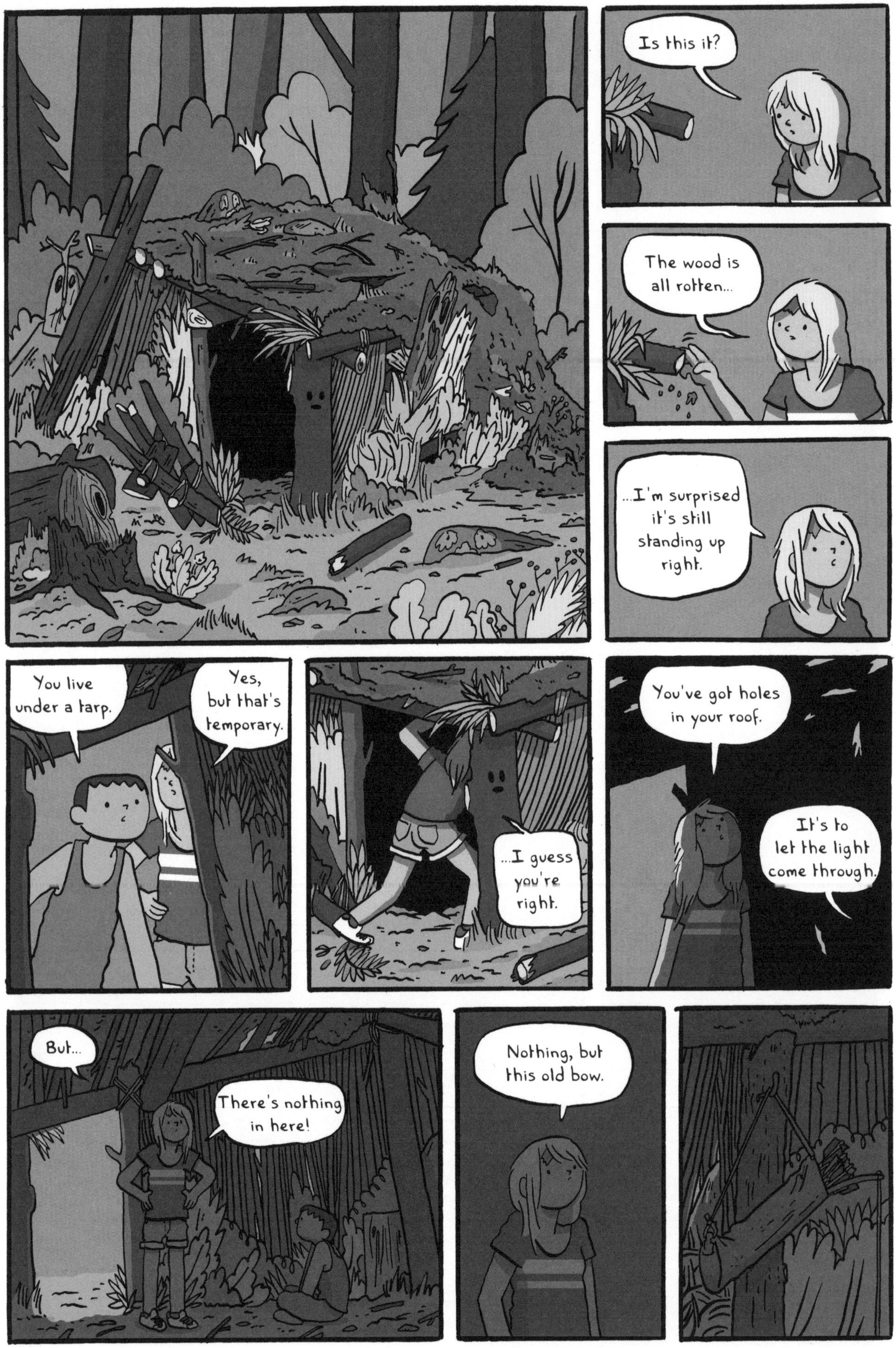
Is this it?
The wood is all rotten...
...I'm surprised it's still standing up right.
You live under a tarp.
Yes, but that's temporary.
...I guess you're right.
You've got holes in your roof.
It's to let the light come through.
But...
There's nothing in here!
Nothing, but this old bow.

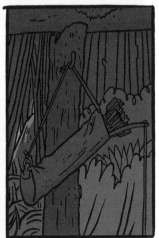

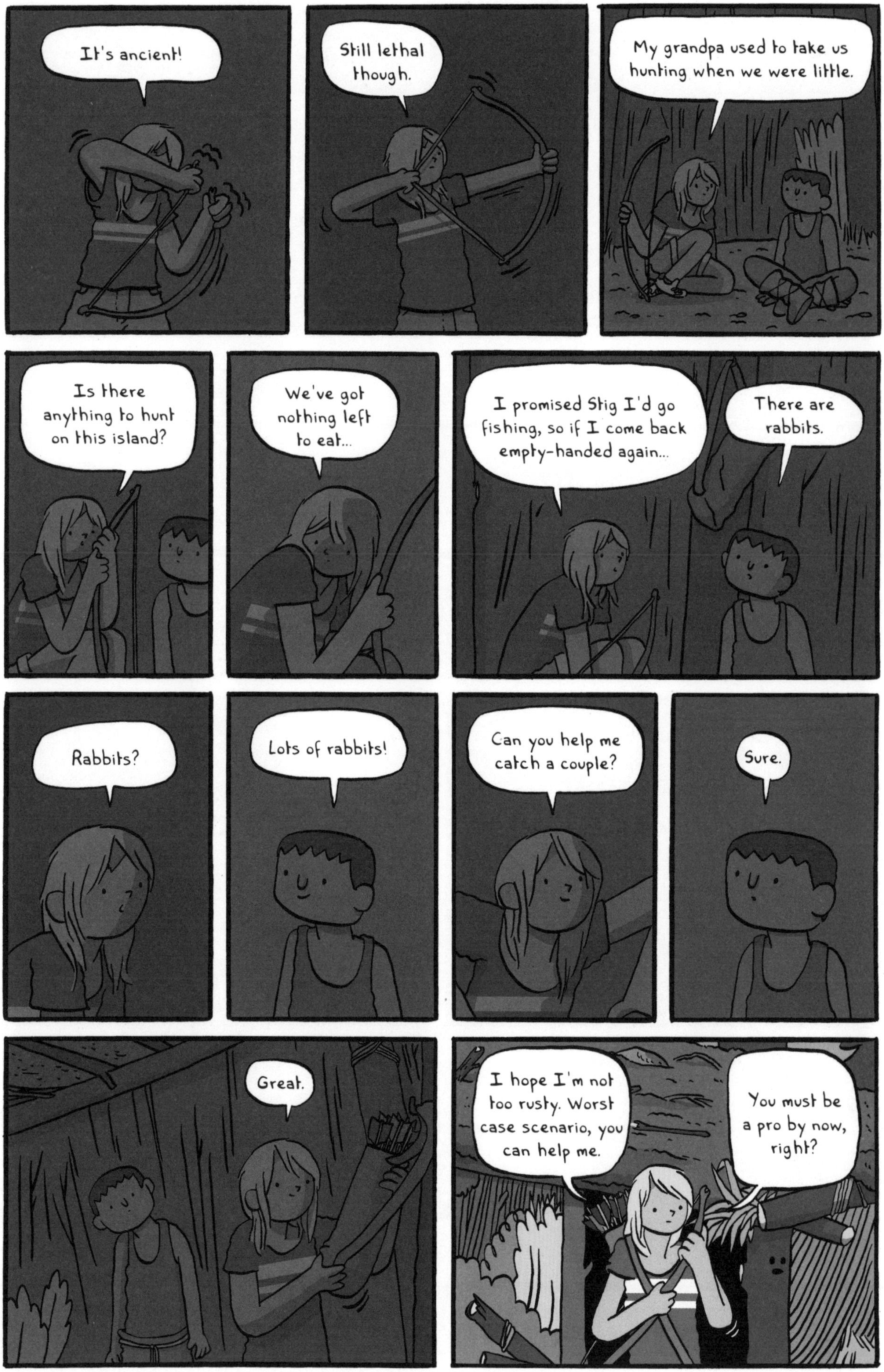
It's ancient!
Still lethal though.
My grandpa used to take us hunting when we were little.
Is there anything to hunt on this island?
We've got nothing left to eat...
I promised Stig I'd go fishing, so if I come back empty-handed again...
There are rabbits.
Rabbits?
Lots of rabbits!
Can you help me catch a couple?
Sure.
Great.
I hope I'm not too rusty. Worst case scenario, you can help me.
You must be a pro by now, right?

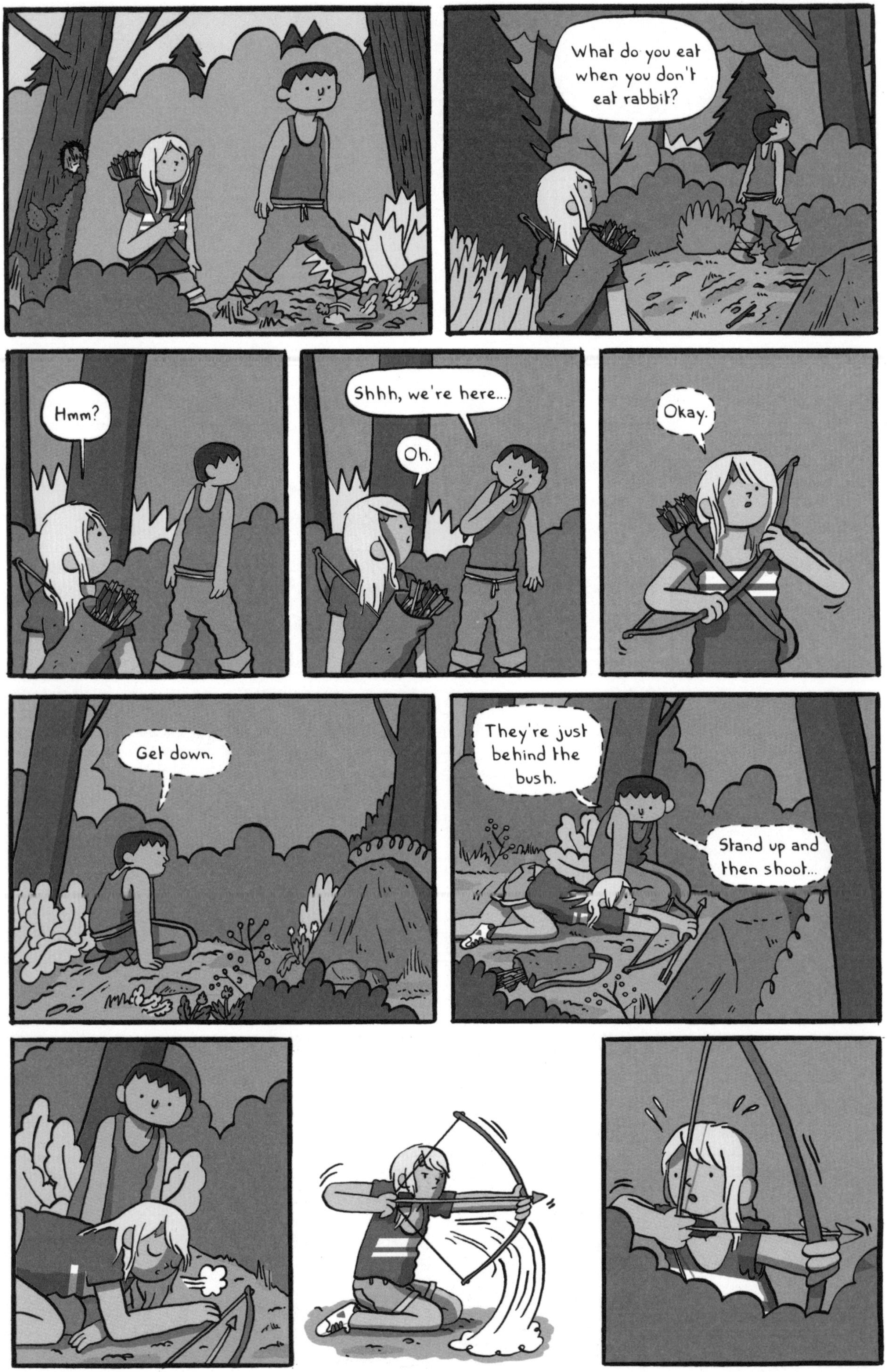
What do you eat when you don't eat rabbit?
Hmm?
Shhh, we're here...
Oh.
Okay.
Get down.
They're just behind the bush.
Stand up and then shoot...

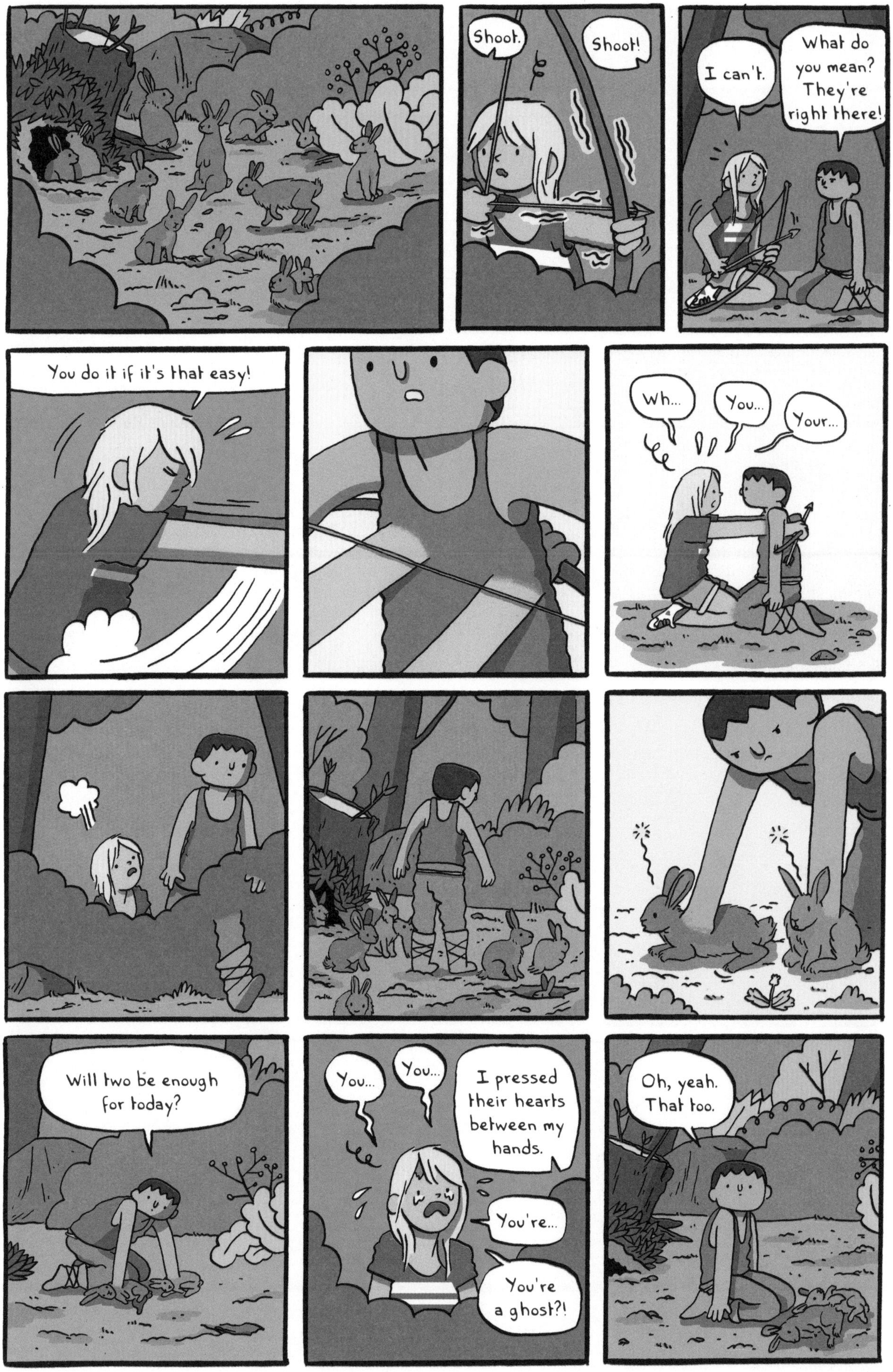

Shoot.
Shoot!
I can't.
What do you mean? They're right there!
You do it if it's that easy!
Wh...
You...
Your...
Will two be enough for today?
You...
You...
I pressed their hearts between my hands.
You're...
You're a ghost?!
Oh, yeah. That too.

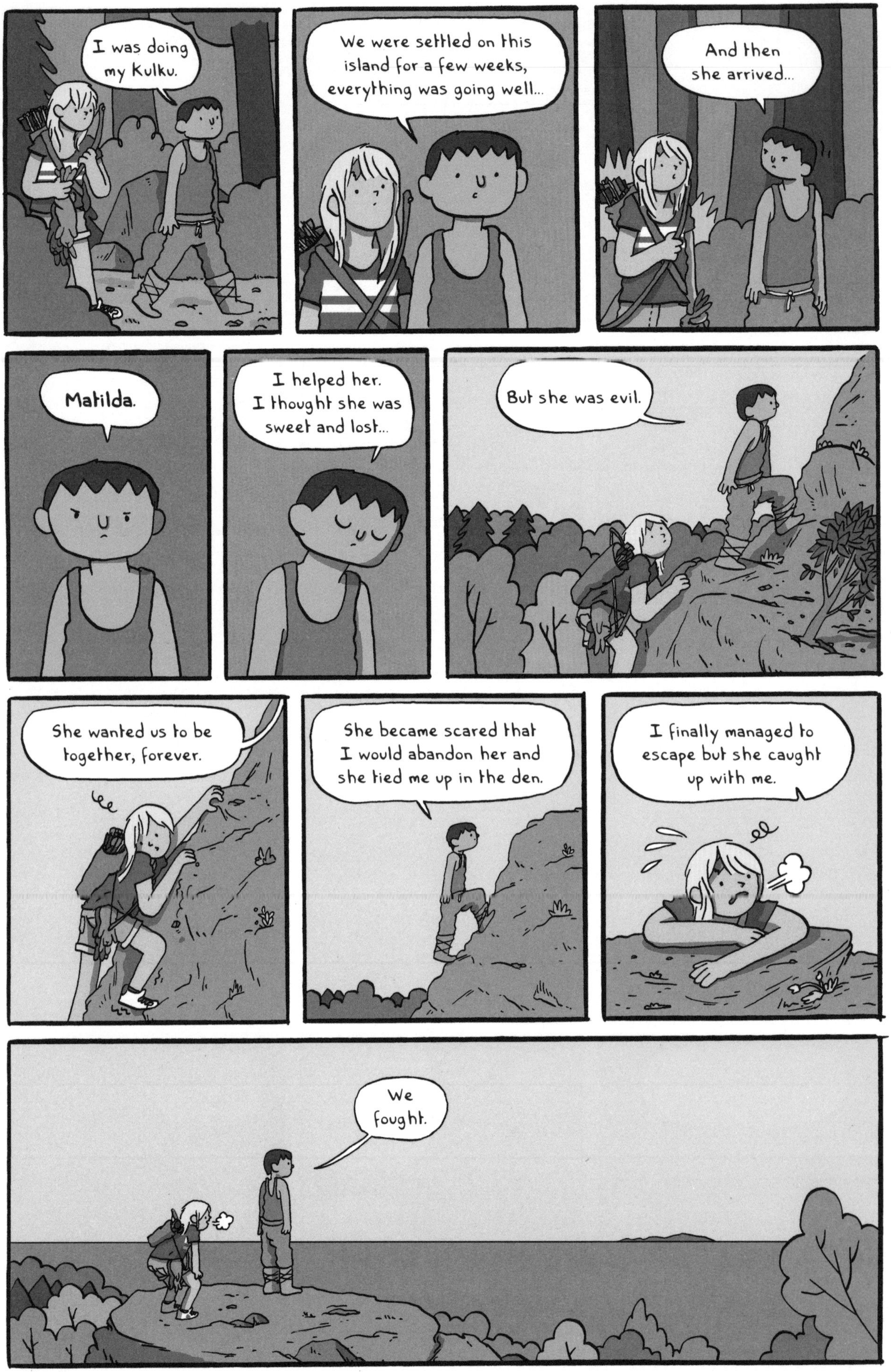
I was doing my Kulku.
We were settled on this island for a few weeks, everything was going well...
And then she arrived...
Matilda.
I helped her. I thought she was sweet and lost...
But she was evil.
She wanted us to be together, forever.
She became scared that I would abandon her and she tied me up in the den.
I finally managed to escape but she caught up with me.
We fought.

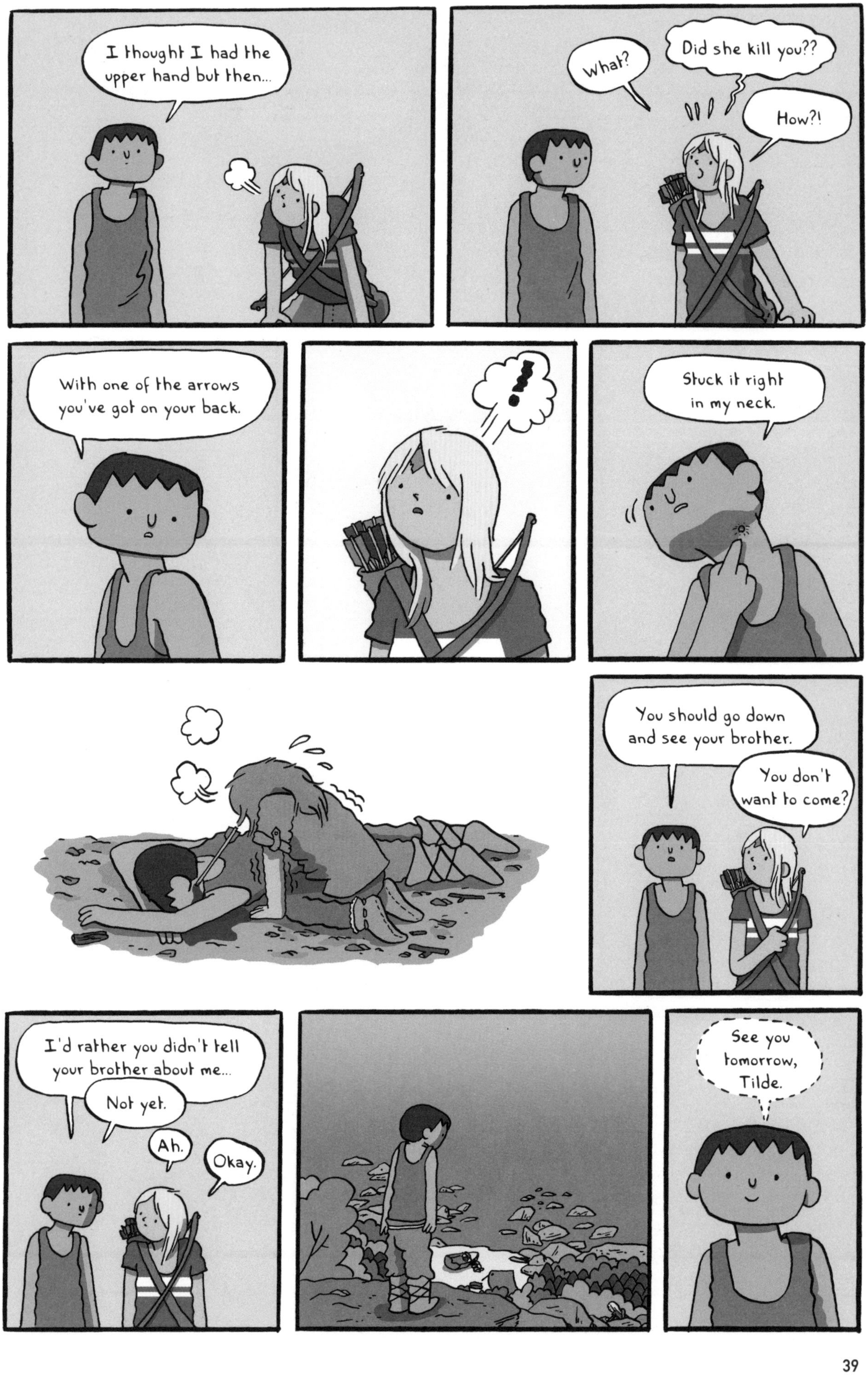
I thought I had the upper hand but then...
What?
Did she kill you??
How?!
With one of the arrows you've got on your back.
Stuck it right in my neck.
You should go down and see your brother.
You don't want to come?
I'd rather you didn't tell your brother about me...
Not yet.
Ah.
Okay.
See you tomorrow, Tilde.

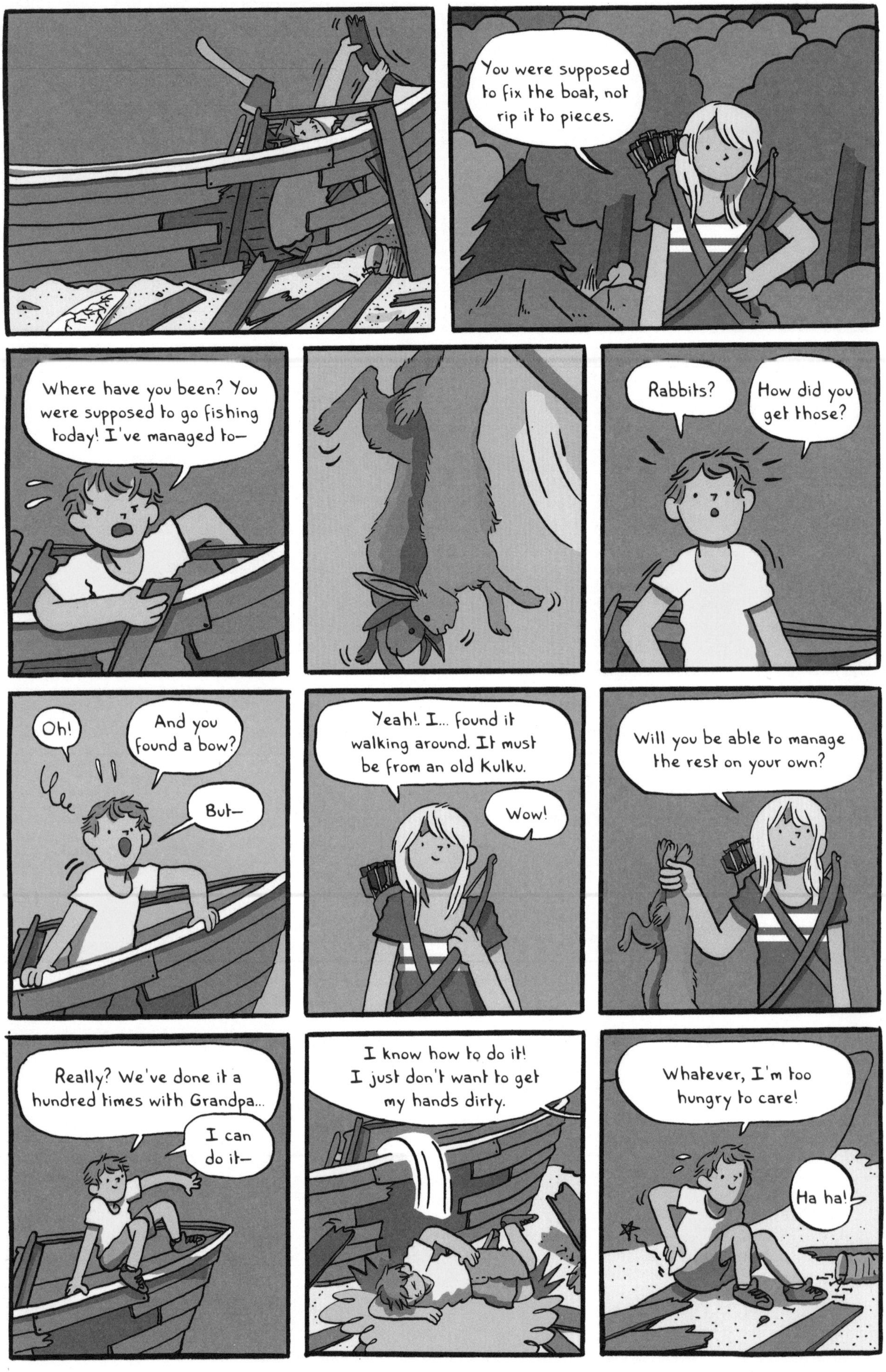
You were supposed to fix the boat, not rip it to pieces.
Where have you been? You were supposed to go fishing today! I've managed to—
Rabbits?
How did you get those?
Oh!
And you found a bow?
But—
Yeah!. I... found it walking around. It must be from an old Kulku.
Wow!
Will you be able to manage the rest on your own?
Really? We've done it a hundred times with Grandpa...
I can do it—
I know how to do it! I just don't want to get my hands dirty.
Whatever, I'm too hungry to care!
Ha ha!

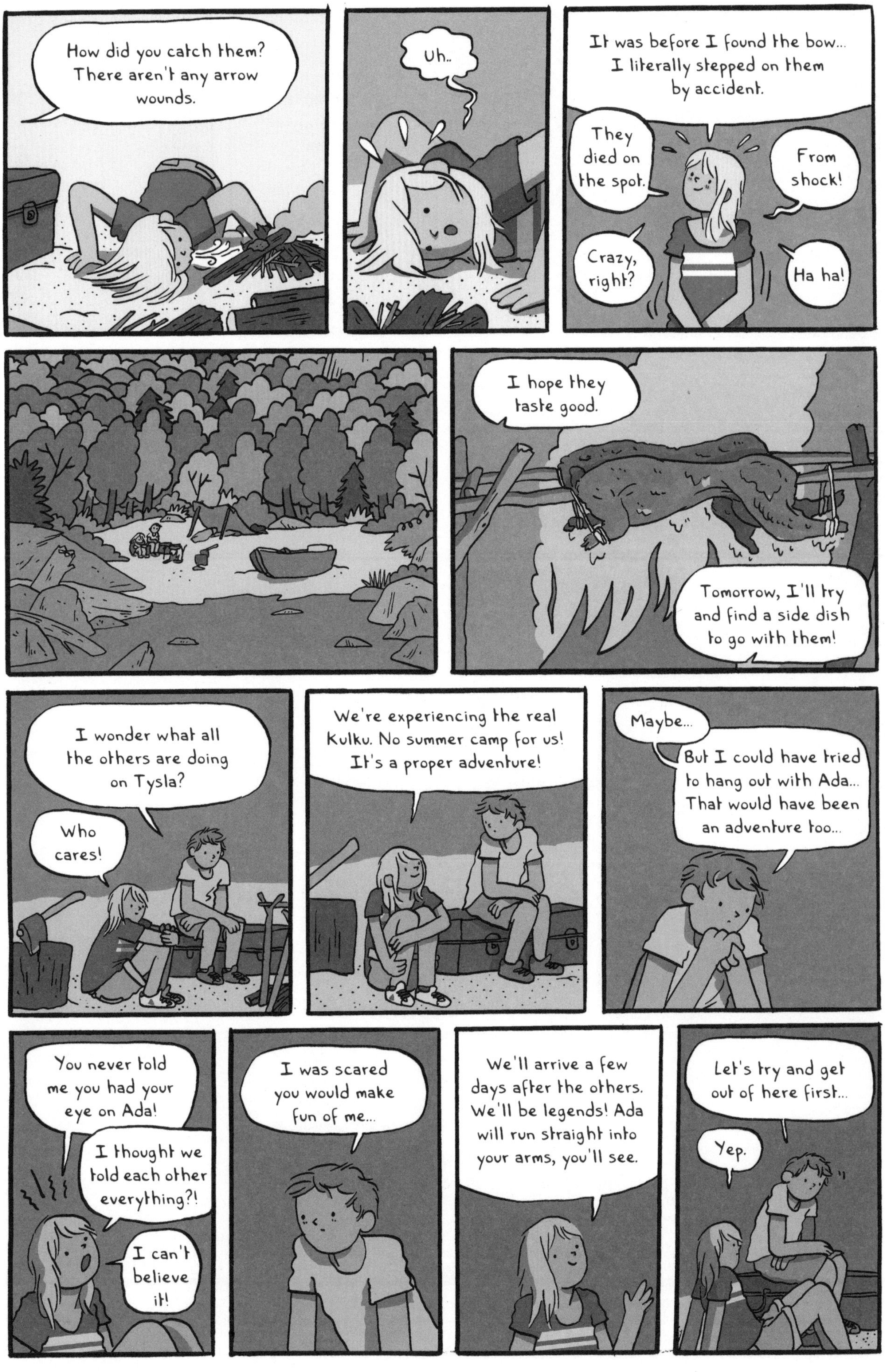
How did you catch them? There aren't any arrow wounds.
Uh..
It was before I found the bow... I literally stepped on them by accident.
They died on the spot.
From shock!
Crazy, right?
Ha ha!
I hope they taste good.
Tomorrow, I'll try and find a side dish to go with them!
I wonder what all the others are doing on Tysla?
Who cares!
We're experiencing the real Kulku. No summer camp for us! It's a proper adventure!
Maybe...
But I could have tried to hang out with Ada... That would have been an adventure too...
You never told me you had your eye on Ada!
I thought we told each other everything?!
I can't believe it!
I was scared you would make fun of me...
We'll arrive a few days after the others. We'll be legends! Ada will run straight into your arms, you'll see.
Let's try and get out of here first...
Yep.

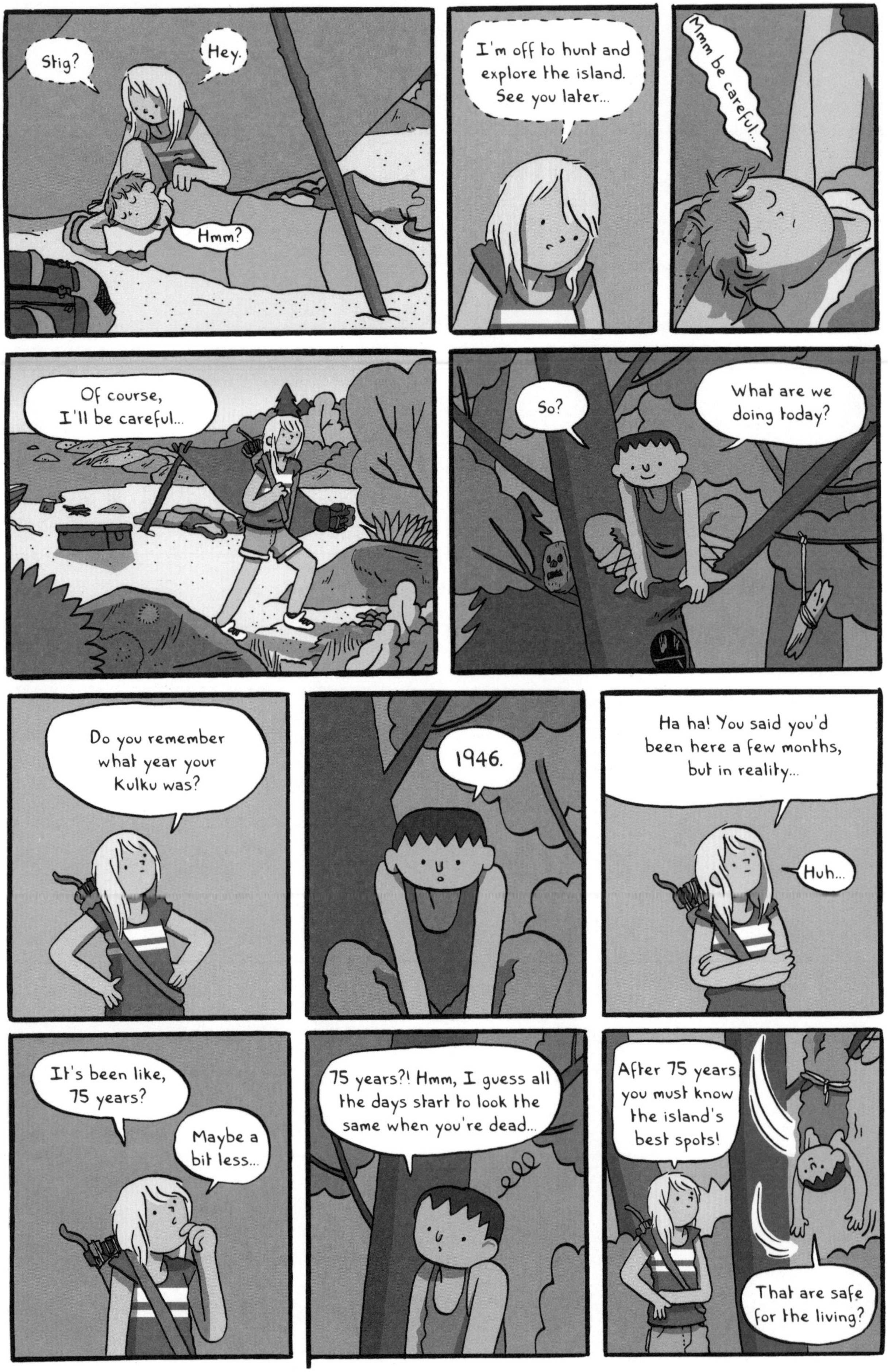
Stig?
Hey.
Hmm?
I'm off to hunt and explore the island. See you later...
Mmm be careful...
Of course, I'll be careful...
So?
What are we doing today?
Do you remember what year your Kulku was?
1946.
Ha ha! You said you'd been here a few months, but in reality...
Huh...
It's been like, 75 years?
Maybe a bit less...
75 years?! Hmm, I guess all the days start to look the same when you're dead...
After 75 years you must know the island's best spots!
That are safe for the living?

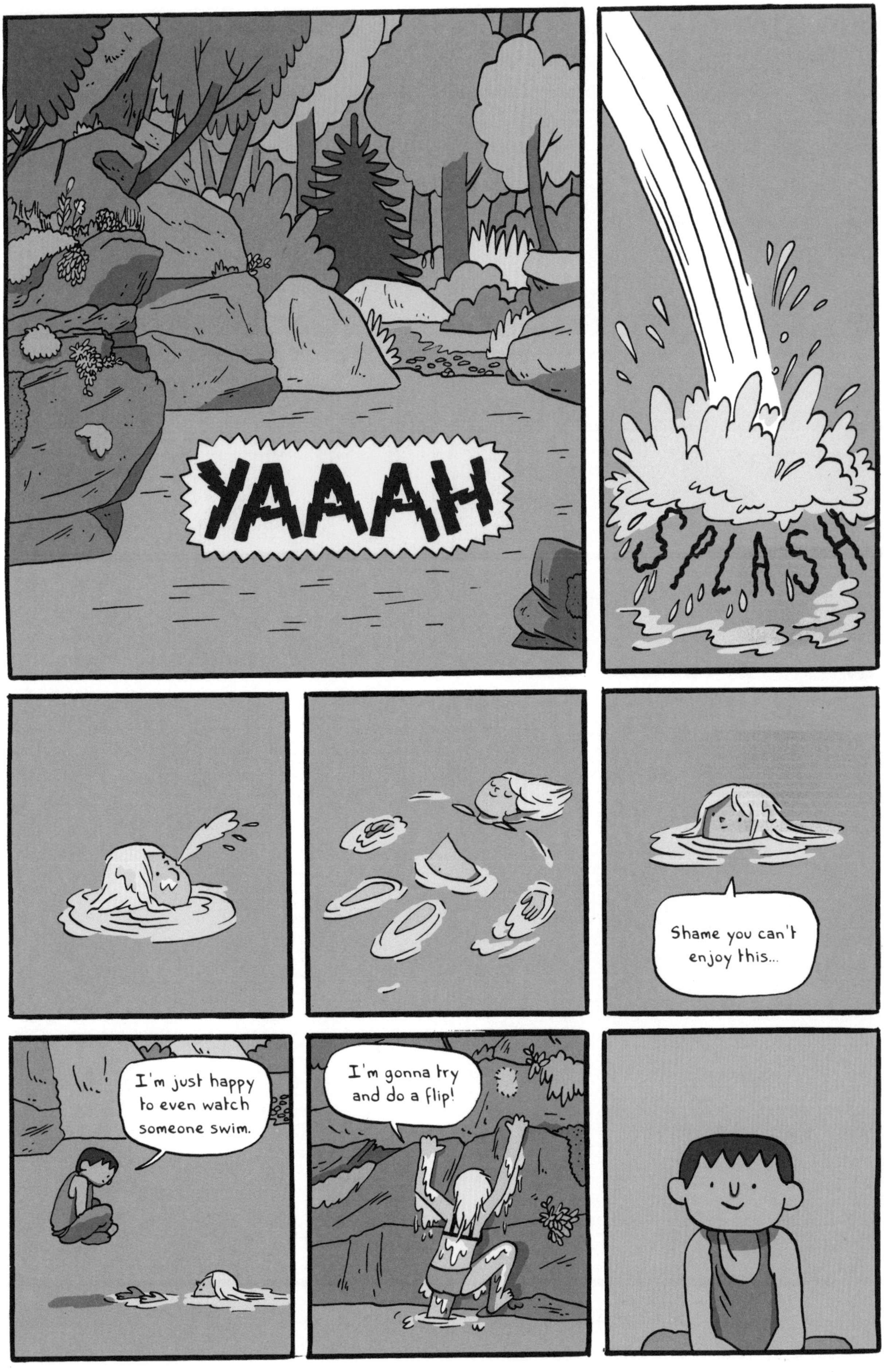
YAAAH
SPLASH
Shame you can't enjoy this...
I'm just happy to even watch someone swim.
I'm gonna try and do a flip!

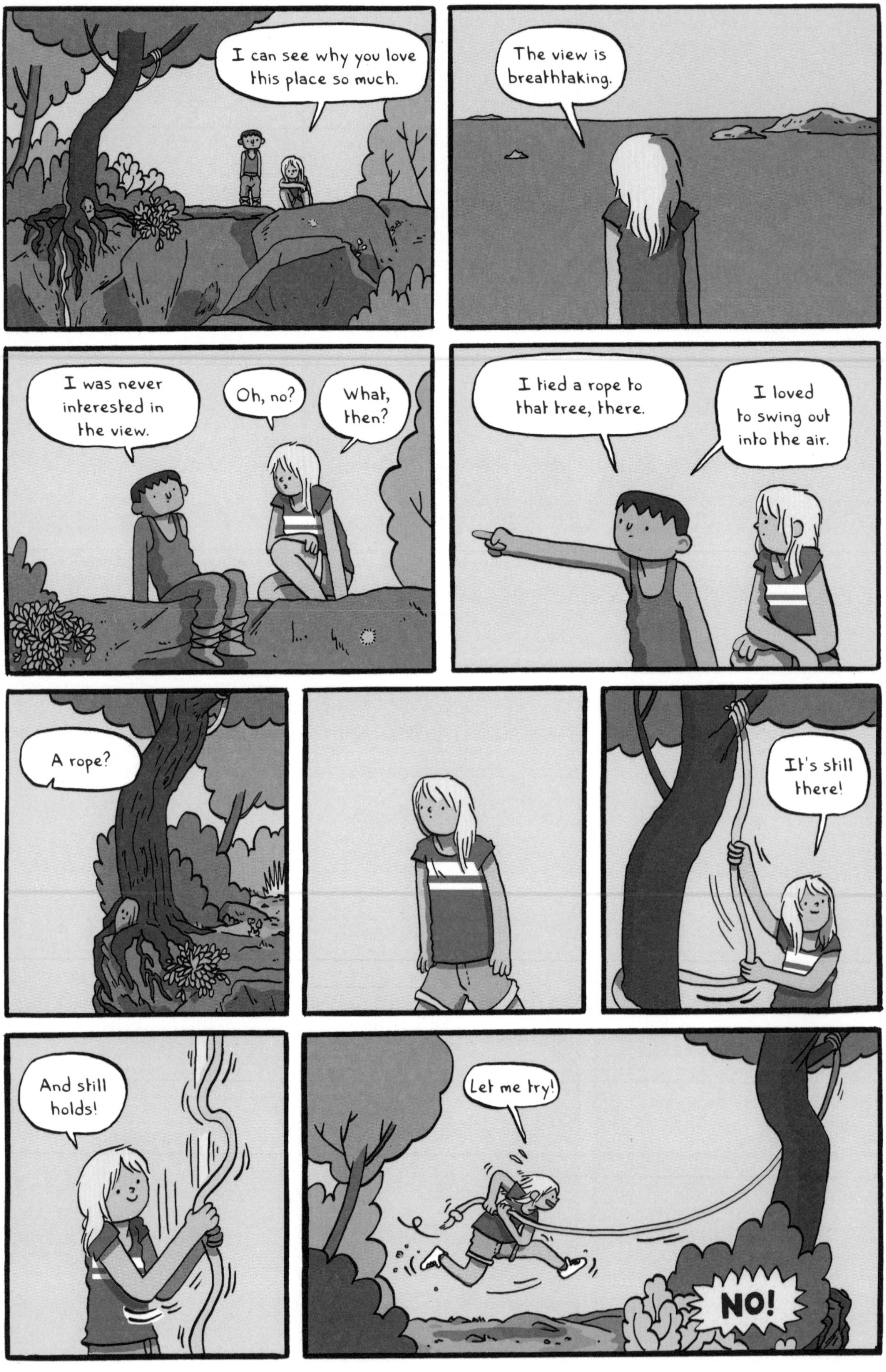
I can see why you love this place so much.
The view is breathtaking.
I was never interested in the view.
Oh, no?
What, then?
I tied a rope to that tree, there.
I loved to swing out into the air.
A rope?
It's still there!
And still holds!
Let me try!
NO!

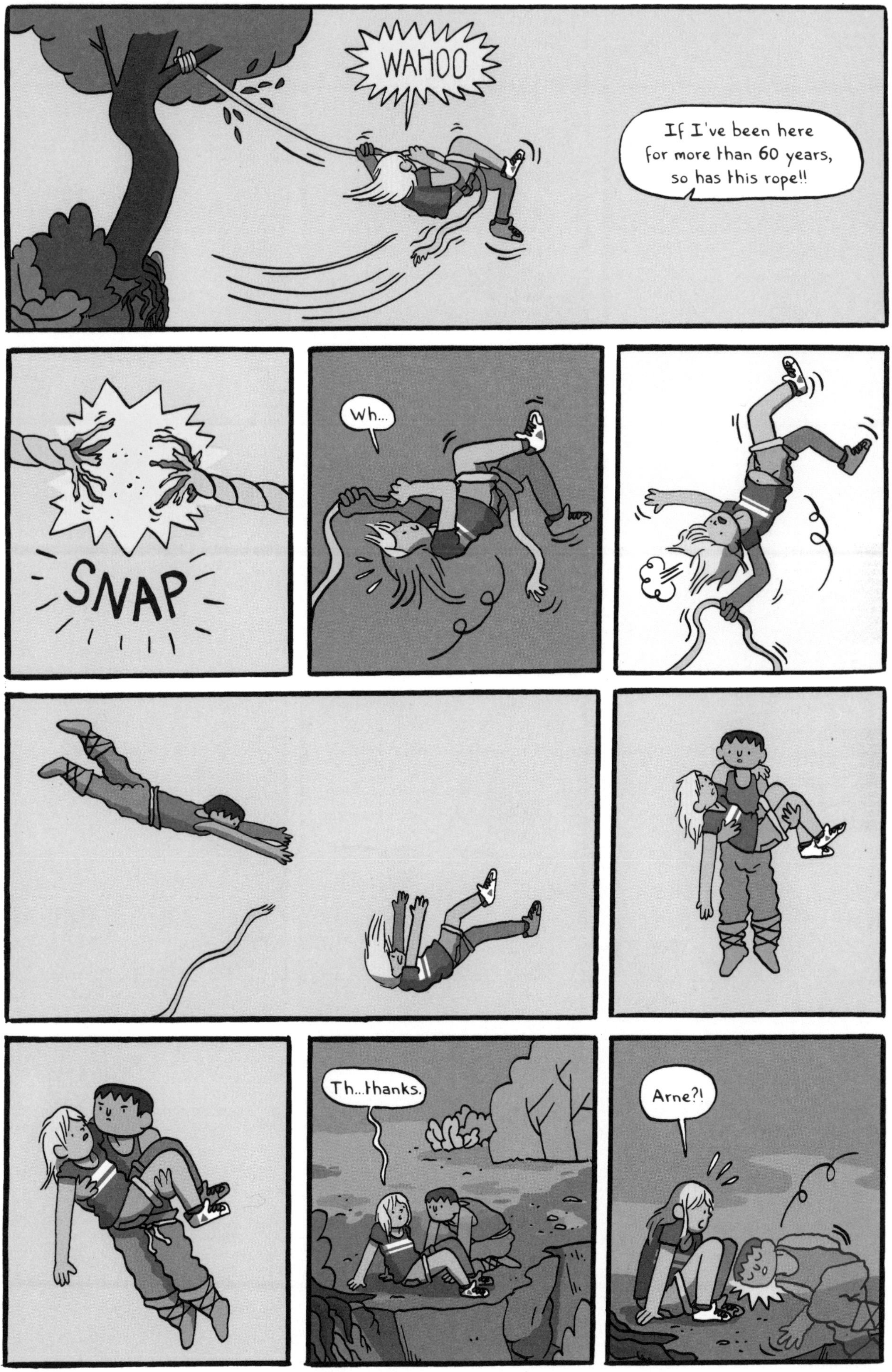
WAHOO
If I've been here for more than 60 years, so has this rope!!
SNAP
Wh...
Th...thanks.
Arne?!

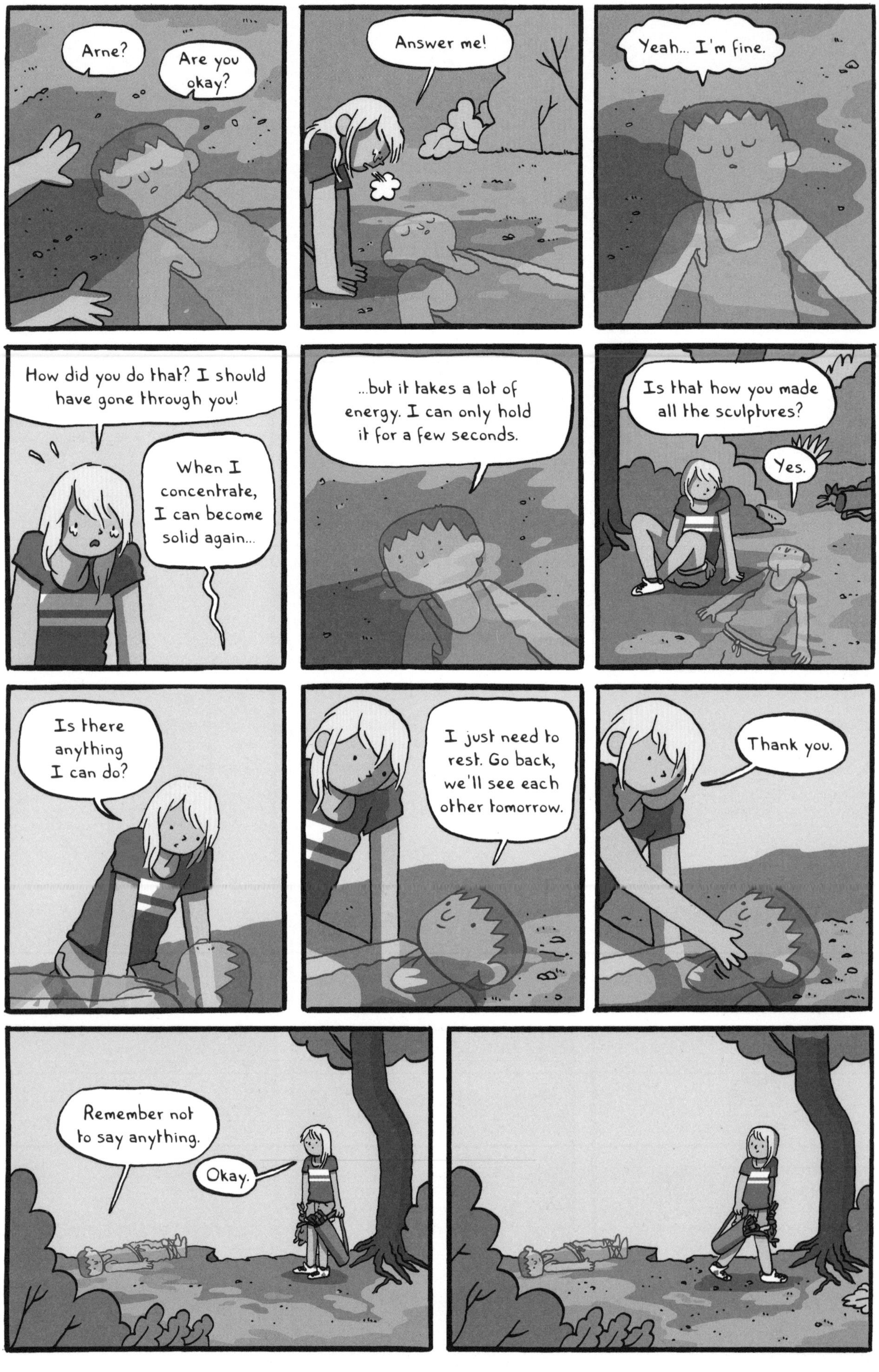
Arne?
Are you okay?
Answer me!
Yeah... I'm fine.
How did you do that? I should have gone through you!
When I concentrate, I can become solid again...
...but it takes a lot of energy. I can only hold it for a few seconds.
Is that how you made all the sculptures?
Yes.
Is there anything I can do?
I just need to rest. Go back, we'll see each other tomorrow.
Thank you.
Remember not to say anything.
Okay.

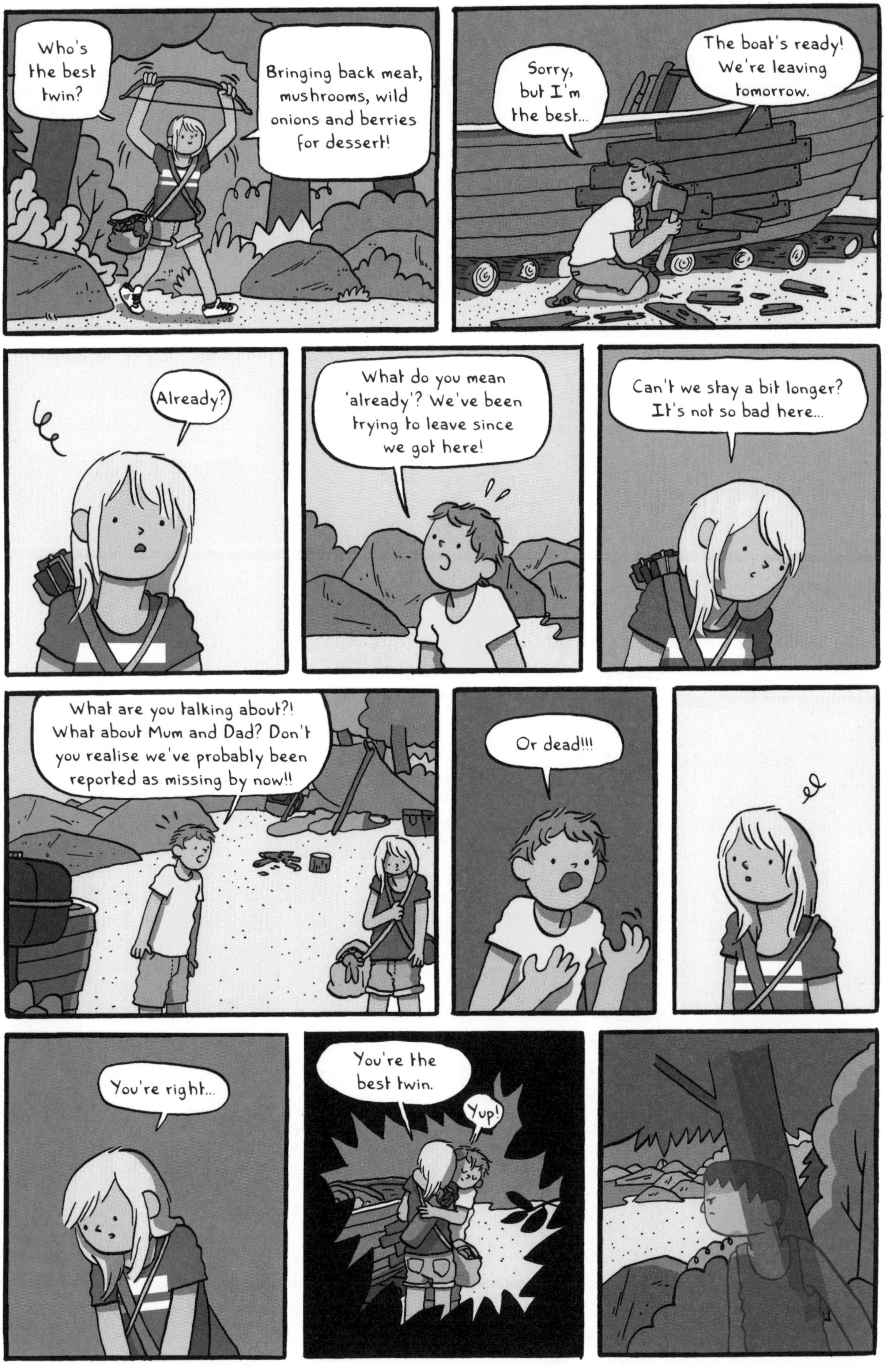
Who's the best twin?
Bringing back meat, mushrooms, wild onions and berries for dessert!
Sorry, but I'm the best...
The boat's ready! We're leaving tomorrow.
Already?
What do you mean 'already'? We've been trying to leave since we got here!
Can't we stay a bit longer? It's not so bad here...
What are you talking about?! What about Mum and Dad? Don't you realise we've probably been reported as missing by now!!
Or dead!!!
You're right...
You're the best twin.
Yup!

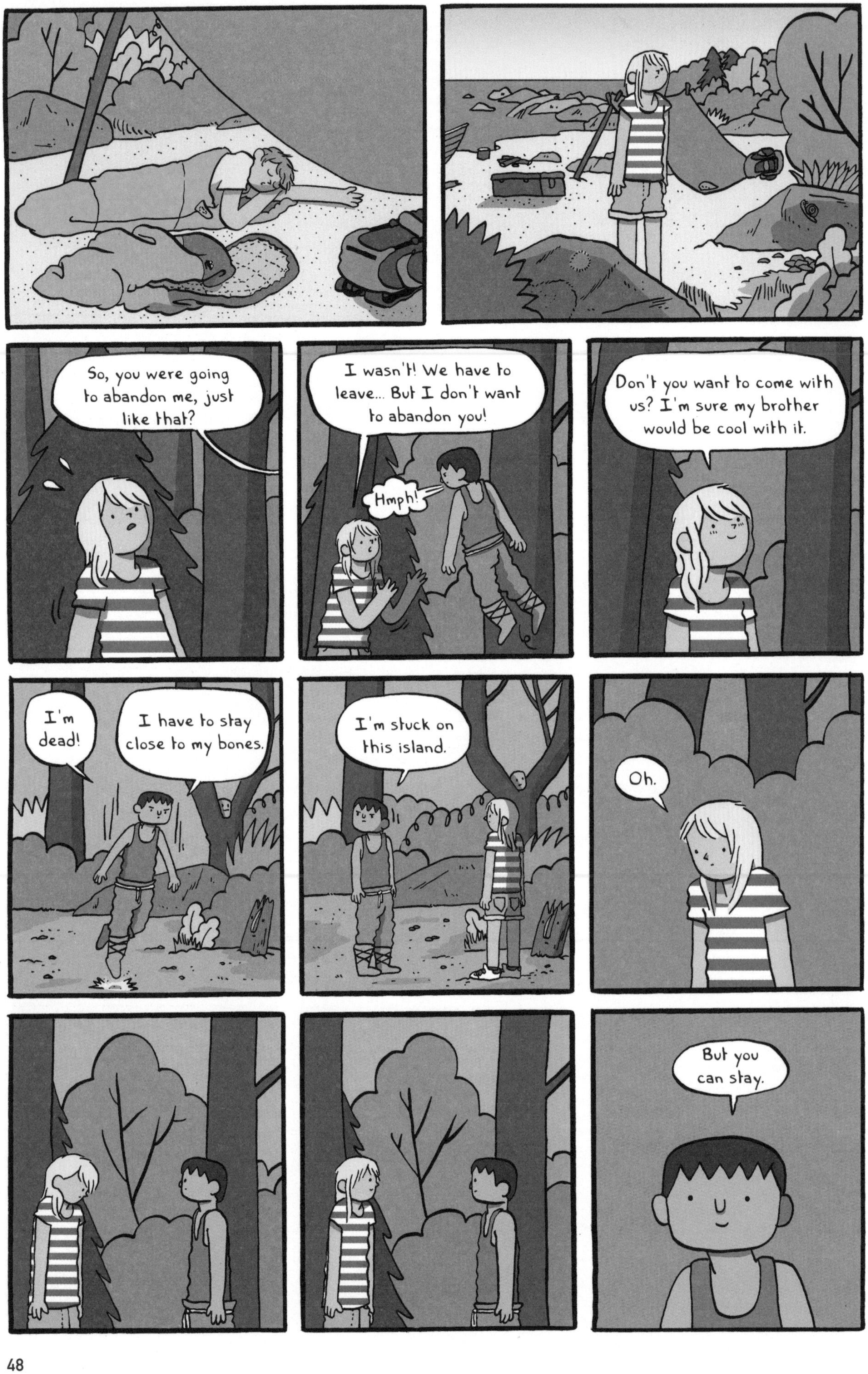
So, you were going to abandon me, just like that?
I wasn't! We have to leave... But I don't want to abandon you!
Hmph!
Don't you want to come with us? I'm sure my brother would be cool with it.
I'm dead!
I have to stay close to my bones.
I'm stuck on this island.
Oh.
But you can stay.

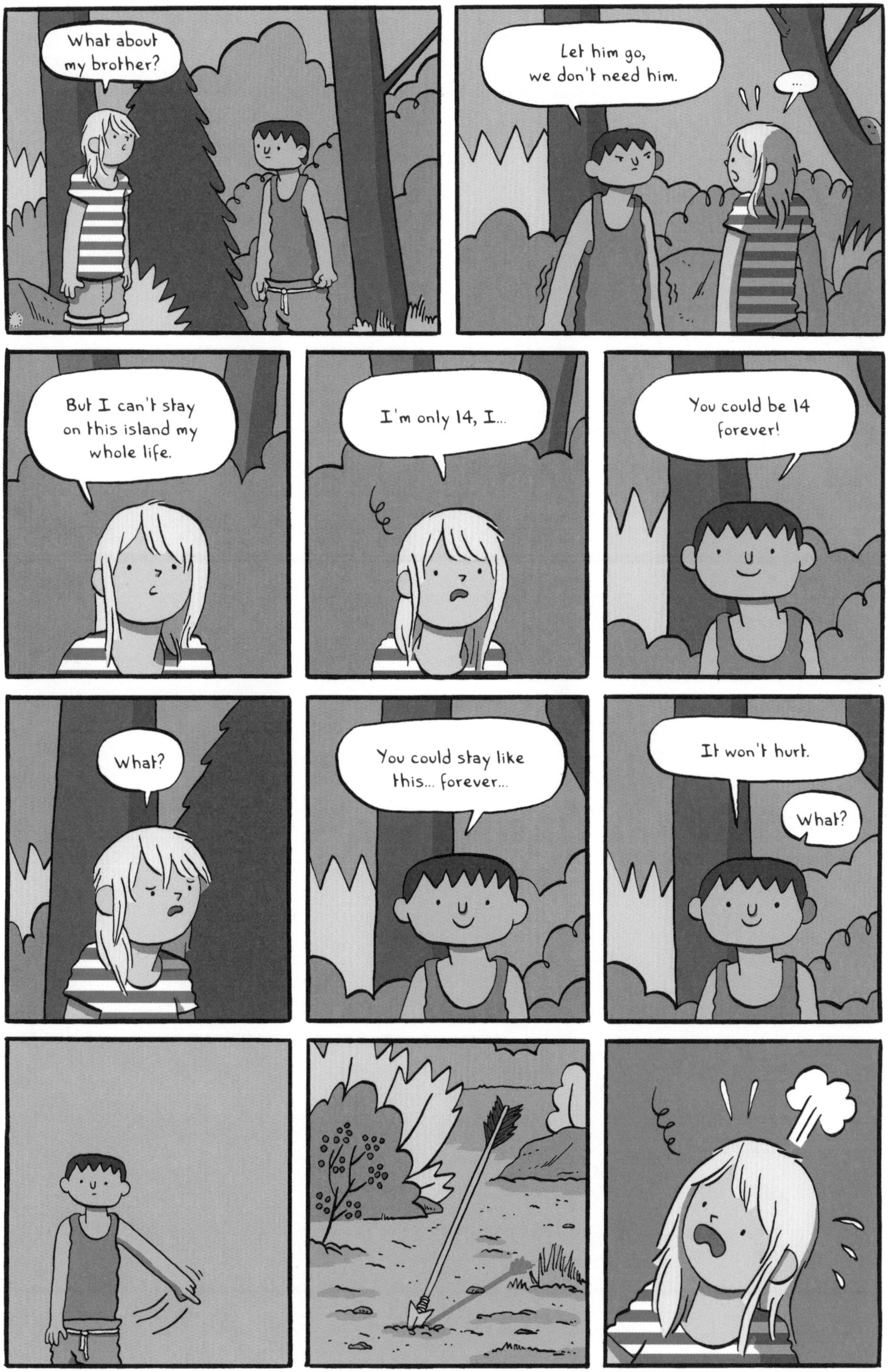
What about my brother?
Let him go, we don't need him.
...
But I can't stay on this island my whole life.
I'm only 14, I...
You could be 14 forever!
What?
You could stay like this... forever...
It won't hurt.
What?

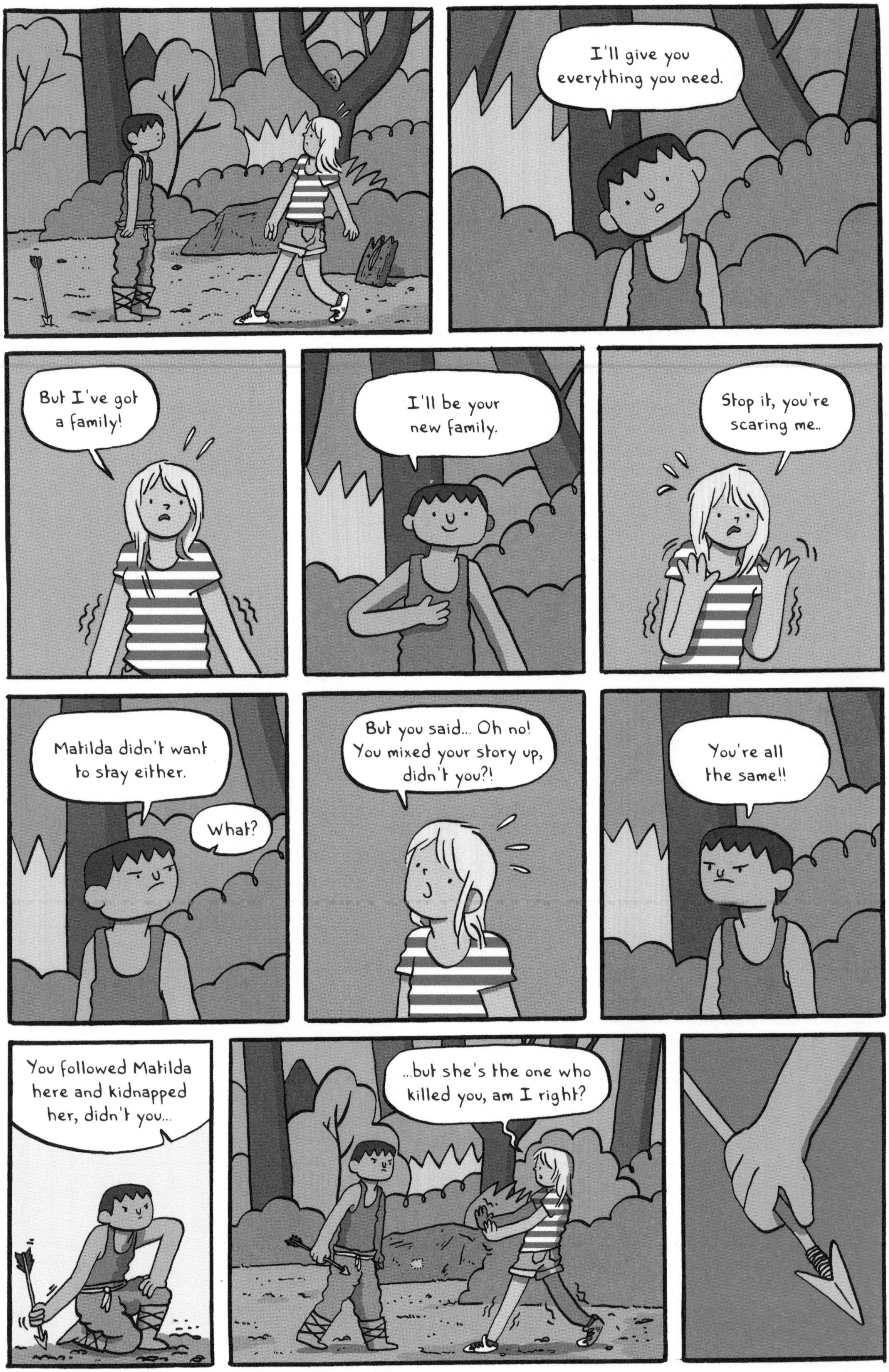
I'll give you everything you need.
But I've got a family!
I'll be your new family.
Stop it, you're scaring me..
Matilda didn't want to stay either.
What?
But you said... Oh no! You mixed your story up, didn't you?!
You're all the same!!
You followed Matilda here and kidnapped her, didn't you...
...but she's the one who killed you, am I right?

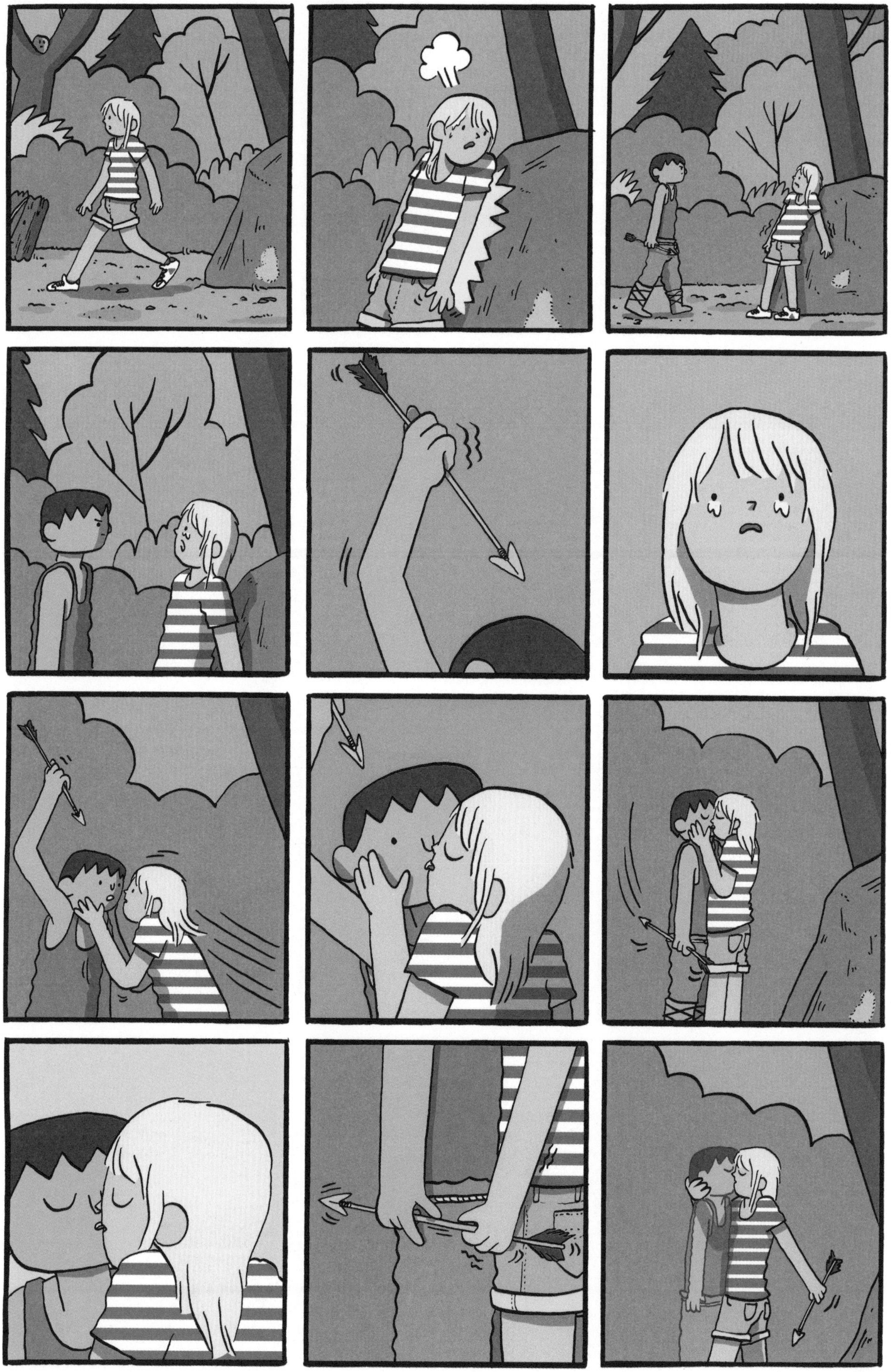

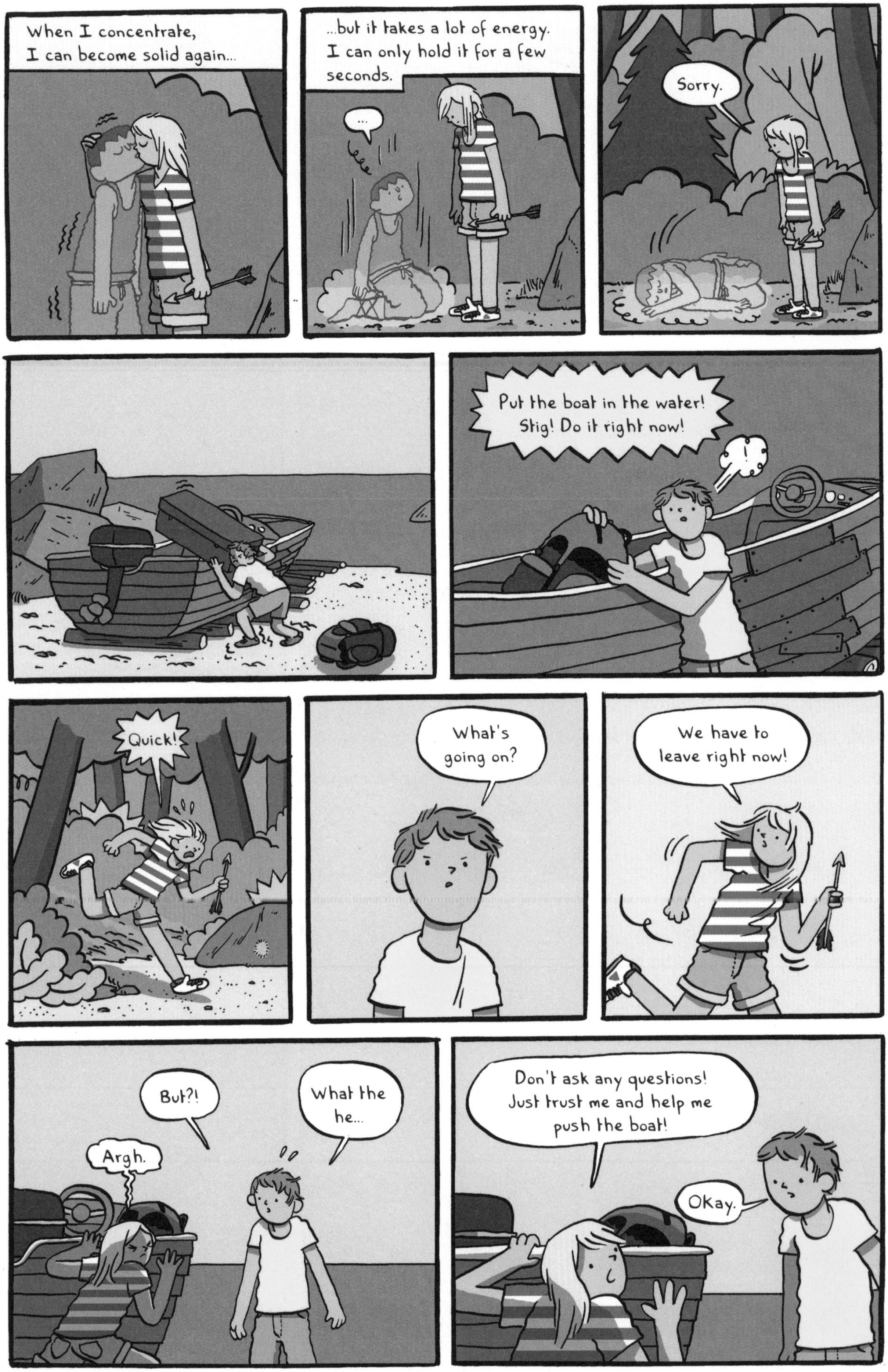
When I concentrate,
I can become solid again...
...but it takes a lot of energy.
I can only hold it for a few seconds.
...
Sorry.
Put the boat in the water!
Stig! Do it right now!
!
Quick!
What's going on?
We have to leave right now!
But?!
Argh.
What the he...
Don't ask any questions!
Just trust me and help me push the boat!
Okay.

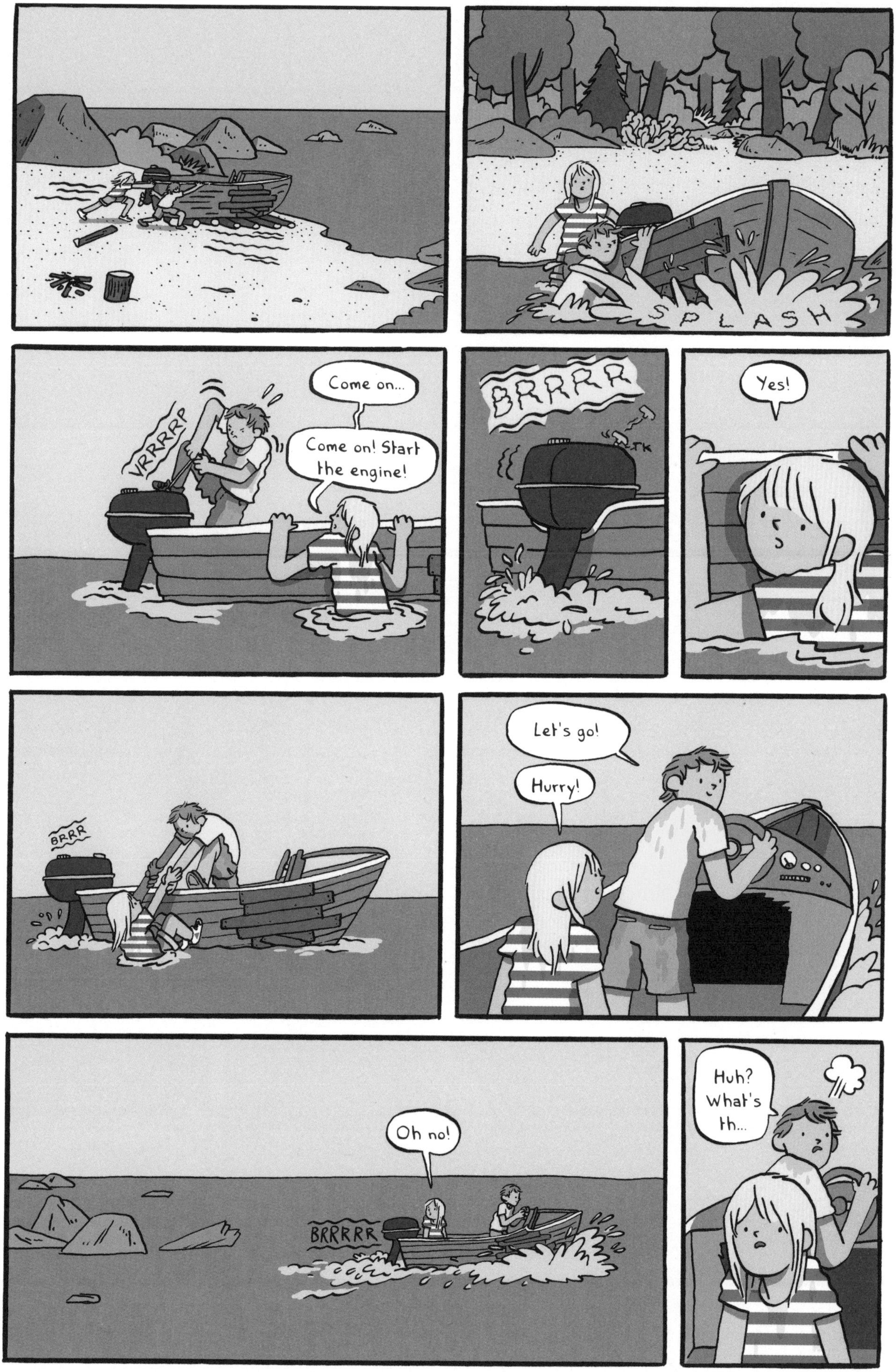
SPLASH
VRRRRP
Come on...
Come on! Start the engine!
BRRRR
TK
Yes!
BRRR
Let's go!
Hurry!
Oh no!
BRRRRR
Huh? What's th...

SWOOSSHHHHHHHHHHH

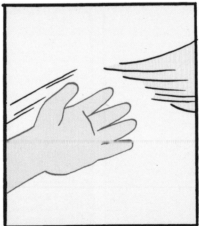

AAAH

TILDE!

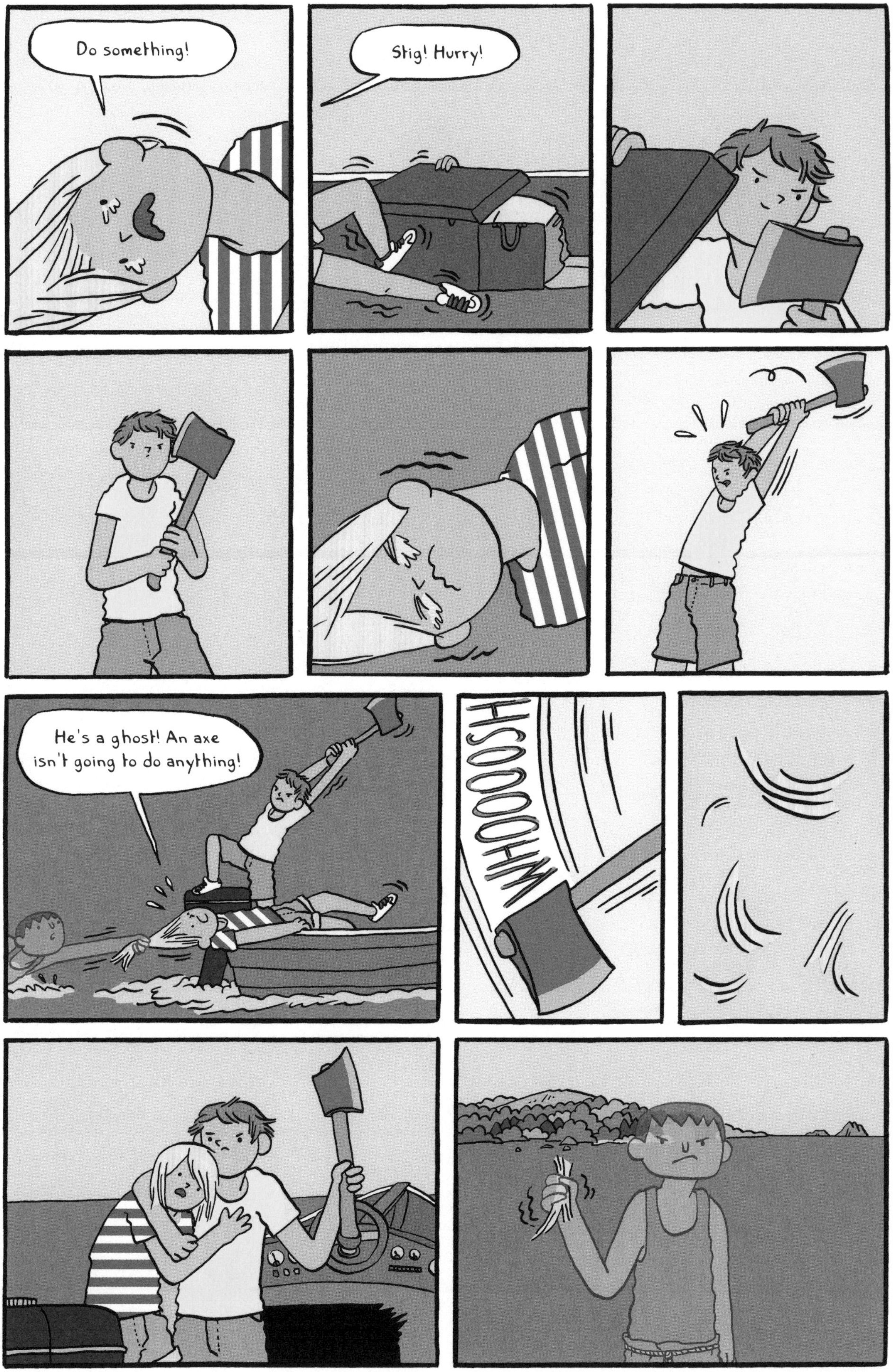
Do something!
Stig! Hurry!
He's a ghost! An axe isn't going to do anything!
WHOOOOSH

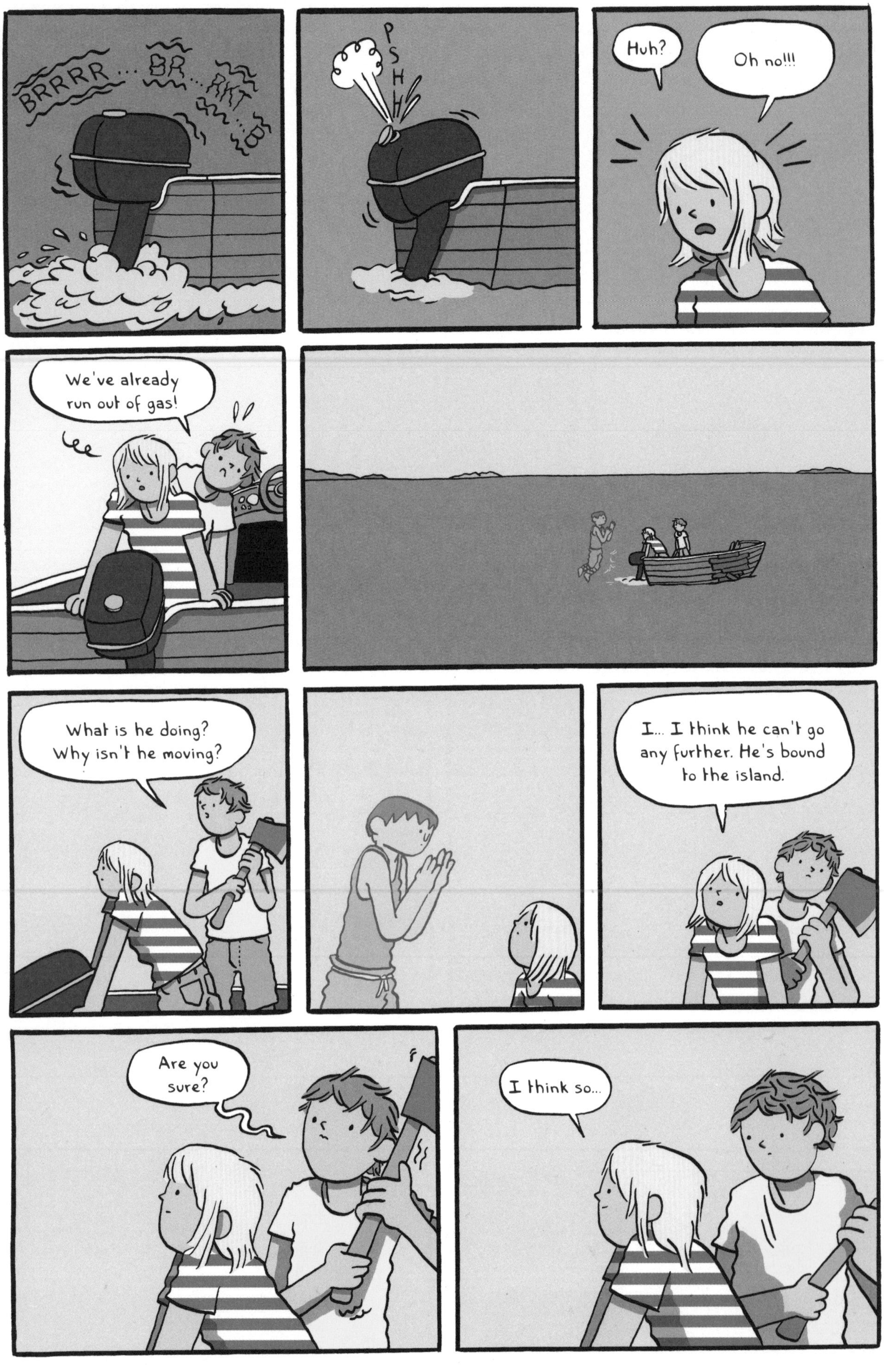
BRRRR... BR... RKT... B
PSHH
Huh?
Oh no!!!
We've already run out of gas!
What is he doing? Why isn't he moving?
I... I think he can't go any further. He's bound to the island.
Are you sure?
I think so...

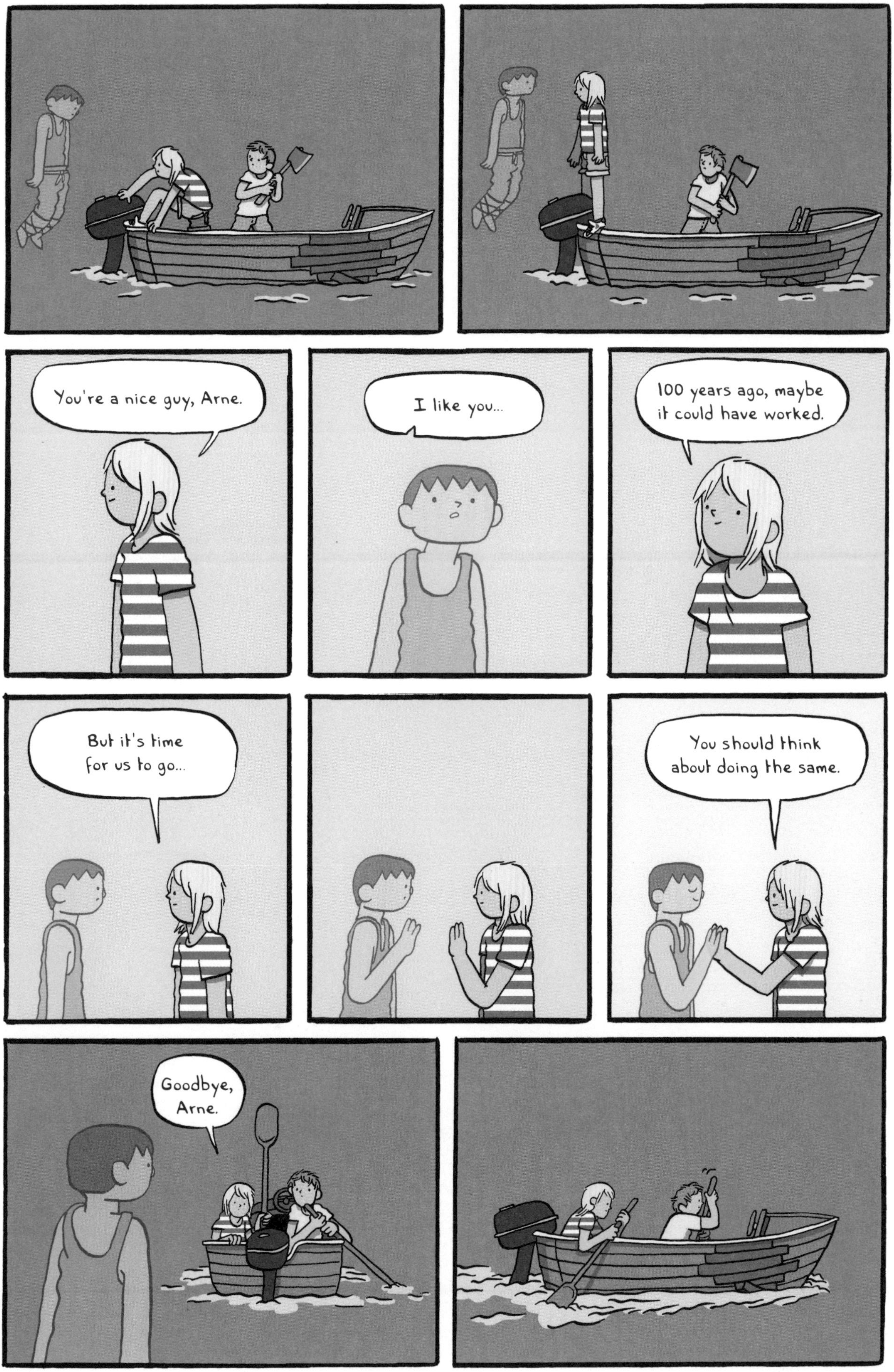
You're a nice guy, Arne.
I like you...
100 years ago, maybe it could have worked.
But it's time for us to go...
You should think about doing the same.
Goodbye, Arne.

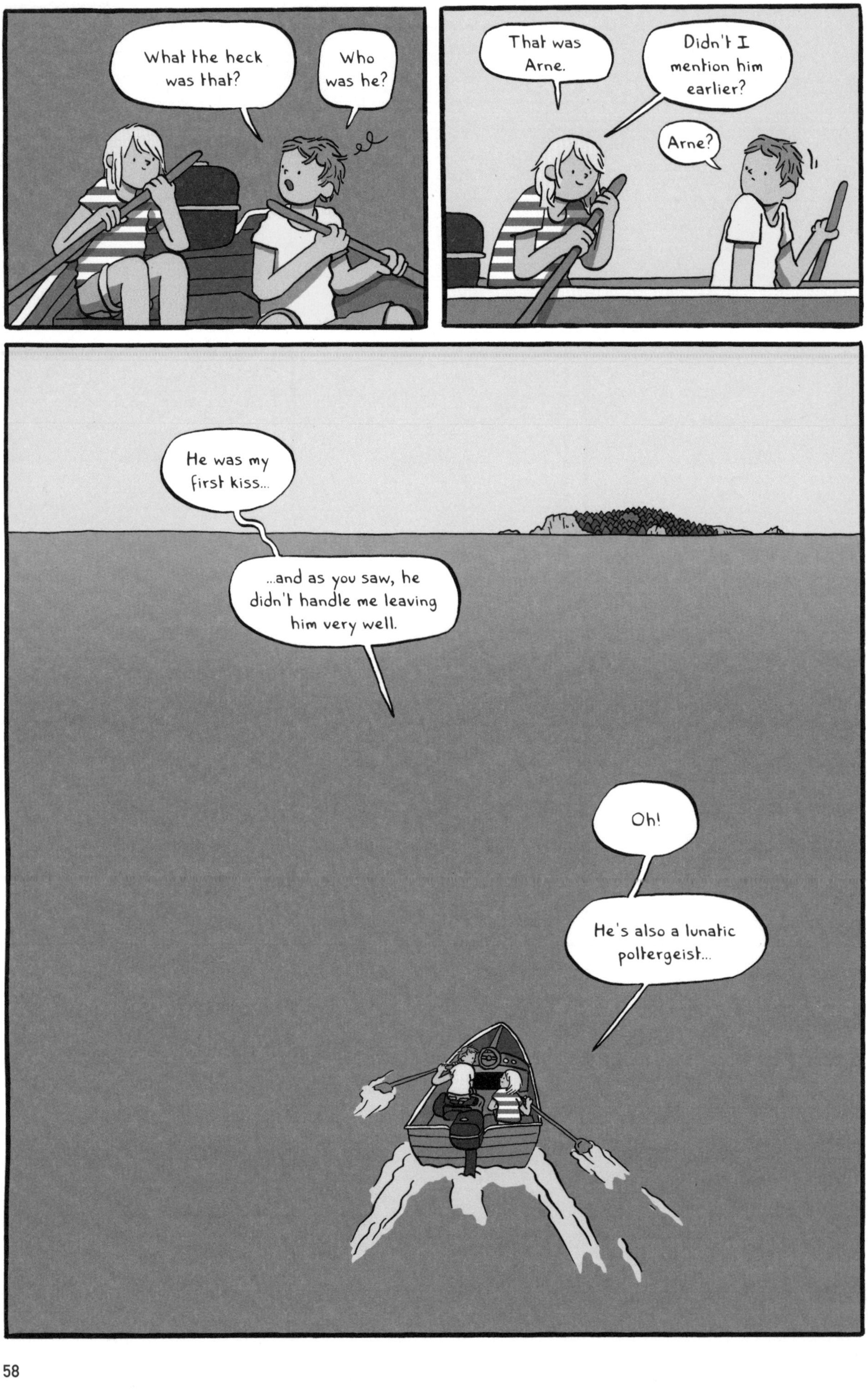
What the heck was that?
Who was he?
That was Arne.
Didn't I mention him earlier?
Arne?
He was my first kiss...
...and as you saw, he didn't handle me leaving him very well.
Oh!
He's also a lunatic poltergeist...